Praise for the ⌐⌐⌐ ⌐y **Baantjer**

"Along with such peers as Ed McBain and Georges Simenon, [Baantjer] has created a long-running and uniformly engaging police series. They are smart, suspenseful, and better-crafted than most in the field."
—*Mystery Scene*

"Baantjer's laconic, rapid-fire storytelling has spun out a surprisingly complex web of mysteries."
—*Kirkus Reviews*

"DeKok is a careful, compassionate policeman in the tradition of Maigret; crime fans will enjoy this book."
—*Library Journal*

"DeKok's maverick personality certainly makes him a compassionate judge of other outsiders and an astute analyst of antisocial behavior."
—*The New York Times Book Review*

"It's easy to understand the appeal of Amsterdam police detective DeKok; he hides his intelligence behind a phlegmatic demeanor, like an old dog that lazes by the fireplace and only shows his teeth when the house is threatened."
—*The Los Angeles Times*

"A major new voice in crime fiction for America."
—*Clues: A Journal of Detection*

Other Inspector DeKok Mysteries
Now Available or Coming Soon

DeKok and the Geese of Death
DeKok and the Death of a Clown
Murder In Amsterdam

DeKok and Murder by Melody

by
A. C. Baantjer

Translated by H. G. Smittenaar

speck press
denver

Book layout and design by: *CPG,* corvuspublishinggroup.com
Printed and bound in the United States of America

ISBN: 0-9725776-9-6, ISBN13: 978-0-9725776-9-4

English translation by H. G. Smittenaar copyright © 2005 Speck Press. Translated from *DeCock en de moord op melodie,* by Baantjer (Albert Cornelis Baantjer), copyright © 1983 by Uitgeverij De Fontein bv, Baarn, Netherlands.

Library of Congress Cataloging-in-Publication Data

Baantjer, A. C.
[De Cock en de moord op melodie. English]
DeKok and murder by melody / by A. C. Baantjer ; translated from the Dutch by H.G. Smittenaar.
p. cm.
ISBN 0-9725776-9-6
1. DeKok, Inspector (Fictitious character)--Fiction. I. Smittenaar, H. G. II. Title.
PT5881.12.A2D56513 2005
839.31'364--dc22
2005008302

10 9 8 7 6 5 4 3 2 1

TRANSLATOR'S NOTE

Truth being stranger than fiction, most of Baantjer's stories are based on his own experiences as an officer of the Amsterdam Metropolitan Police (thirty-eight years, twenty-five years in homicide). But this particular story is based on actual events from before World War II and adapted for more recent times. Baantjer joined the police force in June 1945, one month after the war ended.

AMSTERDAM

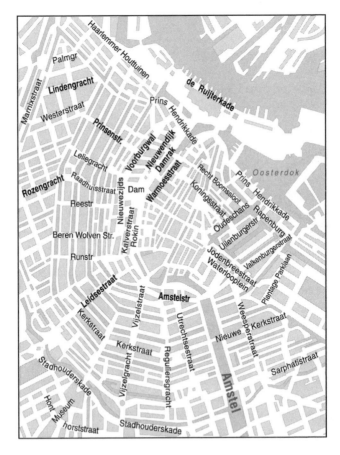

1

Jean-Paul Stappert waited at the curb in front of the clearly marked pedestrian crossing. He locked his eyes on the oddly stylized, red figure in the pedestrian light across the street. To his left and right people passed, ignoring the crossing light. He reflected it was actually a bit strange the little scarlet man in the light diverted his attention, causing him to freeze to the curb. Less than a year ago he would have crossed without thinking, just like the other pedestrians. He would probably not even have lifted his head to look at the light, would have ignored the traffic as well.

Once he had a close shave with a truck. He crossed at the last possible moment; the truck clipped him on the shoulder. He was not so much hurt as startled and knew it was his own fault. The driver didn't even notice. But Jean-Paul stood on the sidewalk for several minutes, stamping his feet and cursing in rage.

He could hardly imagine behaving as he did. He had definitely changed. He was certainly mellower. Life was better going with the flow. He found people more tolerable—some were almost likeable.

He felt himself begin to change one day when he suddenly heard, deep in his subconscious, the sound of an oboe playing a lovely melody. It was an early, crisp winter morning. He was busy trying to break the lock of a parked car. The memory of this event lingered in his memory. He could evoke the events in perfect detail. He had been lured by the expensive camera on the back seat of the car, seemingly abandoned by a careless motorist.

When he heard the sounds in his head, he replaced the jimmy in his pocket and leaned against the car to listen to the ethereal sound of the oboe. The warm, clear tones moved and affected him in a way he had never before experienced. When he closed his eyes, he heard a playful clarinet take over the theme of the oboe. It was soon joined by the majestic tone of a bassoon. As if from a distance, he heard the tones swell, mingle, and then harmonize into an enchanting melody. He listened, enraptured.

He moved away from the car and leaned against an elm on the side of the canal, where he stared up at the gray sky through the bare branches. The flow of the music mimicked the branches of the tree. Phrases ran parallel, criss-crossing, but always striving toward the light. The music ended in a dazzling crescendo. Dazed, he shook his head.

That's how it began. He glanced a second time at the expensive camera, but he was no longer interested. He walked away from the tree, down to the end of the canal. Every once in a while he stopped. He placed his thumbs against the sides of his head and entwined his fingers before his eyes. The music would reappear, stronger than before. In a strange, almost hypnotic state he eventually found his way home.

Back on the street the traffic light changed; the static, little red man was replaced by the green silhouette of a walking man.

Jean-Paul stepped off the curb and crossed the road. On the other side of the Damrak, near the terrace of the

Victoria Hotel, he turned left onto the wide sidewalk. It was bustling with the usual strolling tourists and passengers striving toward the Central Station. Sometimes they bumped him. He merely murmured a soft "sorry," and continued on toward the shop windows.

There weren't as many people walking near the buildings. He stopped to look at his watch. With a start he realized it was just ten minutes shy of ten o'clock, later then he had realized. He increased his pace. He did not want to be late, not this time.

Almost at the end of the Damrak, he turned right into Salt Alley, crossed New Dike, and entered Count Street. With a short sprint he crossed just in front of a streetcar on Rear Fort Canal headed toward Mole Alley and reached Lily Canal via Tower Locks.

The sprint winded him a bit. He took a few deep breaths and started to breathe easier. Then he turned toward Emperor's Canal.

Suddenly he stopped. An inner voice told him to stop right then and there. The voice was inexplicable, but irresistible. He became agitated. He looked at his watch. Ten o'clock. He was on time.

Suddenly his hands shook and he felt his heart race. He was overcome by an irrational fear. Sweat beaded on his forehead and trickled down his back. From deep in his subconscious shreds of youthful night terrors surfaced.

He narrowed his eyes and peered into the falling darkness. A bit further down the canal, near the trees on the edge, he could just discern some vague shapes. They seemed to float nearer. For just a moment he hesitated. Then he walked on … toward his death.

Inspector DeKok of the old, renowned police station at Warmoes Street, felt restless. He was editing an extensive report for the judge-advocate, but was unable to concentrate. Vledder, his young colleague and friend, had done most of the actual typing, based on DeKok's suggestions. Vledder, himself, had gathered a wealth of data, storing it in his computer. Now DeKok was supposed to scan it a last time, before he submitted the final report.

With a tired gesture he pushed the pile of papers aside. He stood up and with slow, sluggish steps, began to pace up and down the crowded detective room. Without conscious effort he avoided the obstacles in his path. The other occupants of the room hardly looked up as DeKok paced back and forth in his typical shuffle. DeKok tried to rid himself of a restless uncertainty. Something was bothering him, but he couldn't quite grasp it. Slowly he realized it would be impossible to get rid of the feeling by walking.

He went over to the window and looked out, rocking up and down on the balls of his feet. Diagonally across the street, on the corner of the alley, a drunk carefully navigated his way in the direction of Rear Fort Canal. DeKok smiled. It was fascinating, if slightly pathetic, to watch the man's desperate attempt to proceed in a straight line. He managed it by stopping every time he was about to veer off course. With great effort he would take another two or three steps in a straight line and then stop again, as if recalculating his bearings. His progress was painfully slow.

When the man had finally disappeared from his field of vision, the understanding smile disappeared from DeKok's face. The deep lines around his mouth froze. The restless feeling returned, this time, more intense. It was as if some strange, outside influence was attempting to drive his thoughts into a particular direction. It hovered at the edge of his awareness. He tried to isolate and dissect the feeling, but the key to the code was missing. He was at a loss. His sensitivity, his perception, and understanding of the feelings, was inadequate. An irritating feeling of discomfort gradually engulfed him. He turned around and looked at the clock.

It was two minutes past ten o'clock.

Erik Bavel leaned forward. He turned the key and pulled open the small door of an old sideboard. From behind a large stack of books he produced an electric percolator and placed it on the table. From a gray, earthenware jug, he poured water into the reservoir, and then pushed the plug into the outlet. He extracted a bag of coffee and a paper filter from his leather briefcase. Carefully he measured the amount of coffee.

A mischievous grin flashed across his smooth, young face. "Aunt" Mina Lyons, his avaricious boardinghouse keeper, forbade her tenants to cook in their rooms. They were not even to make coffee—it drove up the electric bill. That is why Erik carefully hid his supplies and coffee pot. Only after ten o'clock at night, when he knew Mina had gone to bed, did he dare to make coffee. Perhaps because it was forbidden, the coffee brewing brought some of the happiest moments of his young life.

When the percolator made its final gurgle, he poured his first cup. A calm sense of satisfaction washed over him. His eagerness and ambition had returned. He was healthy again, cheerful, almost elated. The attacks of depression

that plagued him had abated. His studies had progressed sat-
isfactorily during the last few months. If he could maintain
his pace, he would graduate in about two years. He owed it
all to Jean-Paul, who had guided him and helped him shake
off his depression.

With the mug close by he settled himself comfortably in
an old easy chair with a tall, wide backrest. He picked up a
library book; rather than a textbook, this was an adventure
story. He needed this diversion; the latest round of exams
had been grueling. He slid farther back into the chair.

The book was well crafted and had a lively plot. Right
from the first page Erik was absorbed in the story. He
finished his coffee, but did not pour himself a second mug.
He was so engaged he did not hear the door open, nor did
he notice the figure creeping up behind him.

Young Bavel only became aware of the apparition as
the hands closed around his throat. The hands could have
been made of steel. Erik struggled to pry them loose, but
the pressure was relentless … merciless and immovable. The
book slid onto the floor.

It had taken Erik several moments to realize the intruder
was killing him. He started to struggle more determinedly.
He tried to push himself up in the chair, away from the
distorted, grinning face above him, away from the throt-
tling grip.

But his efforts were in vain. He simply lacked the
strength. Slowly, inexorably, his resistance faltered, as his
life ebbed away. A leaden resignation crept from behind
his neck to his brain, dulling at once his pain and his fear
of death.

After a long time, the grip relaxed. Erik's body slumped
back into the chair. His retina held a vision of endless green

fields, filled with yellow dandelions and exuberant daisies. Above the field it was blue, a compelling azure.

Inspector Vledder turned away from his computer screen and looked up at DeKok.

"What's bothering you?" he asked. "You're either pacing up and down like a caged tiger, or you have a thousand-yard stare."

DeKok, still in front of the window, shrugged his shoulders.

"It's nothing."

It did not sound convincing. Vledder grimaced.

"Come on, tell me another one, DeKok. I know you better than your wife does. I think you're angry, upset. If you don't want to talk, it's okay."

The gray sleuth shook his head.

"I just have a gut feeling something terrible has happened ... something that concerns us."

Vledder grinned broadly.

"There's always something happening, or about to happen, at Warmoes Street. Usually something that involves us. It's inescapable." He pointed to the pile of papers on DeKok's desk. "Kind of like that report—have you finished it?"

"No."

"Tomorrow is the drop deadline."

DeKok moved away from the window and sat down behind his desk. He had not even heard his partner's last remark. He placed his elbows on the desk and sank his chin into his hands. He stared across the room without seeing anything.

"Do you ever have that?" DeKok asked after a long silence.

"Have what?"

"An instinct somebody is trying to contact you ... along eh, along ... unusual paths of communication."

"Telepathy? Nonsense!"

DeKok looked at his friend, a serious look on his face.

"Somebody," said the older man softly, almost whispering, "somebody needed me during the last hour."

DeKok's remarks made him anxious. Vledder felt a chill up his back. He shied away from intuition, relegating it to the same murky realm as superstition and psychic phenomena. He glanced at the clock to break the tension.

"It's just about eleven. The shift is behind us." He pointed at the pile of papers on DeKok's desk. "Tomorrow we're in it up to our necks. The judge-advocate has already given you several extensions. He won't wait any longer."

DeKok growled. He was used to differences of opinion with his superiors. It hardly touched him. With an impatient gesture he pointed at Vledder's telephone.

"Before we go, call the watch commander and ask if he's had any new reports."

Vledder shook his head, sighing deeply.

"If they need us, they know where to find us." He sounded irked. "Besides," he continued, "I want to go home. This time of night the only thing I want to take on is some supper and the couch."

Suddenly the telephone rang.

Vledder picked up the receiver and listened. He soon replaced the receiver, slowly. His face drained of color.

"What is it," asked DeKok tensely.

"It's a corpse."

"Where?"

"It was found in a boardinghouse at Prince Henry Quay."

"Murder?" asked DeKok evenly.

Vledder stood up and nodded.

"The victim was strangled."

2

DeKok looked at the slumped figure in the easy chair and took off his hat. He believed death was entitled to a certain dignity. This was especially true when death came in such a violent form. He would never get used to it. Every time was jarring. The phenomenon of sudden death had intrigued him since he was first professionally confronted with a corpse. Since that time he had solved many mysteries, bringing many murky, inexplicable cases to resolution with logic and clarity.

DeKok studied the boyish face. Still preoccupied by his earlier feelings he wondered whether this youth had felt death imminent. Was he the one who had sent out the distress signals of fear and confusion DeKok had sensed earlier in the evening? With an effort he cleared his mind of such thoughts, focusing on the facts before him. Vledder looked at his partner.

"Since when do you take off your hat for a junkie?"

It sounded harsh and mocking. But DeKok knew it was Vledder's way of dealing with the sadness and depression that overcame him. A sense of futility overwhelms officers confronted daily with violent death.

"A junkie?" asked DeKok, surprise in his voice. He pointed at the corpse. "He doesn't look like a junkie to me. He's washed and shaved and wears clean clothes."

"Maybe he's kicked the habit," admitted Vledder grudgingly. "But as recently as last year he was a regular in the cells. He did mostly robberies and break-ins, cars and warehouses."

DeKok nodded his understanding.

"You have a name?"

Vledder took a notebook out of his pocket and rifled through the pages.

"I've got him in here, somewhere. I processed the paperwork a few times when he was picked up." He grinned. "The last time he broke into a car with a cop standing just across the street."

DeKok pointed around the room.

"Did he live here then?"

"No." Vledder shook his head. He was home-less—registered at his parents' house, but sleeping in some abandoned building on Monk Street." He suddenly tapped a page. "Here it is, Erik Bavel ... twenty-five ... born in Heemstede."

"Heemstede—that sounds upscale."

"Sure," answered Vledder. "The boy comes from a good family. I met the mother once. She was a real lady. She had come to Warmoes Street to pay her son's bail. Erik was studying medicine at the time, he was also developing a heroin addiction. Mrs. Bavel was very concerned about Erik. She had lost another son, about a year and a half earlier, also because of drugs."

DeKok's face hardened.

"Heroin," he growled grimly. "I'm against the death penalty. But when it comes to merciless dealers who know very well what sort of damage they're doing ... I feel public execution might be a deterrent."

Vledder grinned.

"Careful! That's politically incorrect. Don't let them hear you in The Hague."

DeKok shrugged his shoulders. He leaned closer to the corpse of the young man in the chair. The strangulation marks were clearly visible. It was even possible to detect the individual imprints of the fingers. He had seen the aftermath of strangulations, and knew the pathologist would find broken or crushed cartilage beneath the imprints.

He straightened out and looked at Vledder.

"Who discovered him?"

Vledder pointed a thumb over his shoulder.

"The boardinghouse keeper—she was raging."

"She was naturally upset about the murder!"

Vledder shook his head. He pointed at the percolator.

"No, he had been brewing coffee on the sly."

"What?" exclaimed DeKok, who was accustomed to peculiar reactions from witnesses. This didn't register.

"She forbids it absolutely," said Vledder gravely. "She doesn't want any cooking in the rooms. She's a fanatic on the subject. It uses too much electricity." He nodded toward the corpse. "She suspected the boy was brewing coffee at night, when he was alone. She had smelled an aroma of it in the corridor. That's why she went downstairs tonight, in order to catch him red-handed."

"And when she saw the percolator she became angry?"

"Yes."

"What was her reaction to the dead boy?"

"She appeared untouched." Vledder gave a wry smile. "She acted like it was all an imposition, aimed at her personally. She sounded generally bitter, and refused to give any information about anybody else in the house. When I insisted, she slammed the kitchen door in my face."

"We'll see about that," murmured DeKok.

Bram Weelen, the photographer, came in.

"Good grief, DeKok," he panted, "I was almost in bed. You do pick ungodly hours to summon a person."

The old inspector shrugged his shoulders and with an apologetic gesture, he raised both hands.

"Death," he said in a sepulchral voice, "often makes its appearance during unholy moments."

Bram Weelen placed his aluminum suitcase on the floor, pulled a handkerchief from a pocket, and wiped his forehead. He glanced around the room.

"Anything special you need here?"

DeKok pointed at the suitcase that partially covered the book on the floor.

"Mind the clues."

"Clues, clues," muttered Weelen as he moved the suitcase. "I've never yet spoiled any of your evidence."

"There's always a first time."

"All right, all right all ready."

DeKok turned around. Dr. Koning, the coroner, stood in the door opening. The old man was dressed in his usual 'uniform' of striped trousers, spats, and a swallow-tail coat. In one hand he held his case. In the other was a large Fedora, with a greenish patina, reminiscent of weathered copper. DeKok walked toward the old coroner and welcomed him heartily.

"Were you sound asleep like our photographer?" he asked, pointing at Weelen.

Dr. Koning smiled.

"No, I was on duty tonight, and I have the whole night still before me. From pure boredom I started to read Shakespeare."

"What?"

"MacBeth."

DeKok smiled with admiration.

"Ah, you read real literature."

"Yes," nodded the doctor, "it puts me to sleep."

DeKok shook his head with mild disapproval. He liked Shakespeare; he could not imagine how anyone could find it boring.

Dr. Koning approached the corpse. He placed one hand against the cheek of the victim. Then he pulled up the eyelids. The pupil did not react.

DeKok kept his eyes on the coroner.

"How long has he been dead?"

Dr. Koning did not answer. He straightened up and replaced his hat on his head. He took a small silk handkerchief from a breast pocket and started to clean his lorgnette.

"You know very well, DeKok," he began, "there is little to say about the exact time of death at this point. But the boy is still warm. Based on that, I would venture to say that death may have occurred not too long ago—maybe an hour." He put the handkerchief back in its pocket and replaced the lorgnette. "Did you see the striations?"

"Yes."

"This was done by powerful hands ... somebody who has developed a very strong grip. The murderer could be a tennis player, for instance."

DeKok nodded thoughtfully.

"I'll keep a look-out for him."

The coroner smiled primly.

"It could have been a 'her' as well, you know."

He waved a farewell and went to the door. DeKok called him back.

"Haven't you forgotten something?"

Dr. Koning returned to the chair and bent his head slightly in DeKok's direction. The gray eyes behind the lorgnette sparkled mischievously.

"I know what you mean," he said, pointing at the corpse. "He is dead."

Only now was Erik Bavel officially a corpse.

"Thank you, doctor," said DeKok.

Bram Weelen came to stand next to DeKok, his Hasselblad in hand. Together they watched the eccentric coroner leave. The photographer nudged DeKok.

"I've made all the usual pictures, overall and detail shots of the room and the corpse. When I leave I'll take a shot of the building facade. But that's it, as far as I can tell, unless you can think of anything else."

DeKok thought for a moment.

"Try to get a shot of the face that I can use for identification purposes. I mean, not something that looks obviously dead. I might need it. Then, as far as I'm concerned, you can go back to bed."

"You don't want the pictures first thing in the morning?"

DeKok shook his head.

"Tomorrow afternoon is soon enough." He smiled. "And give my best regards to your wife."

As Weelen made his last pictures, Fred Kruger entered. The dactyloscopist had helped with crime scene investigation for many years. He was close to retirement. He nodded toward DeKok and looked around the room.

"This is all?" he asked in a surprised tone of voice.

"What do you mean?" asked DeKok.

Kruger waved around, indicating the room.

"Everything is so ... eh, orderly. There is no chaos, no damage. Nothing was pulled apart. Even the victim looks neat and tidy." He grinned for just a moment. "You could almost call it a tidy murder."

"A murder is never tidy," DeKok said stoically.

Kruger leaned over the victim.

"Do you know yet, who it is?"

DeKok nodded.

"Erik Bavel, twenty-five, a boy from a good background. Vledder knew him as a heroin addict. He'd processed this youngster a few times."

The fingerprint expert showed doubt on his face.

"Doesn't look like a junkie."

"I said the same thing," smiled DeKok. "That's one of the reasons I want you take his prints. I'd prefer now, but you can also do it tomorrow, before the autopsy. I've had some bad experiences with addicts. And with heroin you encounter the strangest scenarios. I'd like to be on the safe side ... don't want any surprises."

"Regarding the identity?"

"Exactly."

Kruger nodded his understanding.

"I'd better do it now."

Bram Weelen took the flash mechanism off his camera and packed the rest of equipment away in his aluminum suitcase. There was a contented look on his face as he winked at DeKok and disappeared.

Kruger knelt next to the chair with the corpse. He placed his case on the floor, removing a small ink roller. He held the right hand of the victim, bent the thumb slightly, and quickly rolled the ink across the inside of the thumb. Then he took out a metal holder and inserted a blank card into it. With a practiced movement he took the finger-print of the inked digit. DeKok leaned forward as he and his fingerprint man studied the imprint. It was a perfect impression. The loops and swirls were perfect.

Kruger put the card aside and proceeded to repeat the operation on the other fingers of the corpse. DeKok watched with admiration. It was not as simple as it might seem to get useful prints of a corpse.

"You need help?"

Kruger shook his head.

"It's a piece of cake. There is no rigor yet. As a matter of fact, I think he's still warm. The fingers are supple enough." He looked around, a mild accusation in his eyes. "Besides, I'm not exactly doing this for the first time."

DeKok smiled. The old man's pride was justified. He turned around and went over to Vledder, who was sitting at the small desk near the windows. He placed a hand on Vledder's shoulder.

"Found anything?"

Vledder pointed at a large pad of graph paper. It was in the middle of the desk, centered on a rubber desk pad. The paper was well used; only a quarter of the sheets remained of an inch-thick pad. The top sheet was blank, except for the faintly blue, pre-printed grid. There were also vague impressions of lines and dashes, presumably made on the previous sheet before it was torn off the pad.

The impressions in the paper created a crazy quilt of undecipherable images. Vledder pointed at the pad.

"What could he have been using this for? Graph paper?" He repeated the words several times. "I searched, but this is the only graph paper in the room."

"No graphs on the used sheets?"

Vledder shook his head.

"I searched through the text books and his notes. Everything else is on yellow and white legal pads. He had no graph paper anywhere else."

DeKok pulled on his lower lip and let it plop back.

"That's strange," he said slowly. He looked at the pad on the desk. Then he decided, "Let's take it with us. Perhaps they can do something with it in the lab." He shook his head and sighed deeply. "You know, Dick, I have a premonition the death of this young man is just the beginning. I think there are more nasty surprises in store. I wouldn't be sur—" He stopped suddenly and turned around to face a constable as he entered the room with a heavy step.

"They're asking if you're about finished here."

"Who wants to know?"

"Dispatch, they just called me on the radio."

DeKok sounded annoyed.

"What's so important?"

"There's another corpse."

"Where?"

"It's on Emperor's Canal, at the edge of the water, between parked cars. Officers are already there to protect the crime scene."

"Why? What sort of crime?"

"It was a strangulation, That's all we know."

DeKok stared at the constable for a moment.

"And they called you?" he finally asked.

"Yessir, they want you over there as soon as possible."

3

There was little space between the parked cars at the canal's edge. They were parked diagonally with the left front tires up against a low, steel railing. Amsterdam had finally mounted these railings to reduce the number of cars that daily wound up in the canals. They weren't very effective, but had reduced the number of cars that went for a swim to about one a day.

DeKok played his flashlight along the sides of the cars. On the car to his right there were definite streaks in the grime on the doors. The grime had been wiped in a slight curve. The victim, concluded DeKok, must have fallen against the car and then slid down to the ground. He knelt next to the corpse and turned the flashlight on the face. The man looked familiar. He thought he had met him once, spoken to him. He searched his memory, but recognition eluded him.

He turned the head of the corpse to one side and looked at the strangulation marks in the neck. They were almost identical to the marks on Erik Bavel's neck. With difficulty he straightened out in the narrow space. His old knees creaked with the strain. From an upright position he again played the flashlight over the dead face. Then he squeezed away from between the cars and gave the flashlight to Vledder.

"Go take a look," he said. "I think I recognize him."

The young inspector in turn, squeezed between the cars. He was back a few seconds later. He was pale and looked confused. He pointed behind him.

"It's another junkie."

"Do you know him?"

"Yes," nodded Vledder, "Jean-Paul Stappert. Until a year or so ago, he was in the cells at least once a month."

DeKok shrugged.

"He looked familiar."

"You should have recognized him," Vledder gloated. "But you never want anything to do with drug crimes. You're too good for that."

DeKok shook his head.

"No, I'm not too good, just too impatient." He sounded apologetic. "I've actually tried dealing with addicts on occasion. But they are such stupid suspects. There's no way you can have a real conversation with an addict. Most aren't alive anymore … they merely exist. Mentally they're already dead, unreachable."

"That's why you leave it to the younger men," accused Vledder.

DeKok did not answer. As a young inspector he had been saddled with the less pleasant jobs. It was only fair the current generation do the same. With a wry smile he realized he had just classified murders as a more pleasant aspect of the job. He suppressed the thought.

"What do you know about him?"

"Stappert?"

"Yes," said DeKok, irritation in his voice. "Who else are we talking about?"

Vledder made an unsure gesture.

"An addict ... a rabbit. Not really a criminal, although he committed a number of stupid burglaries to get the money for the dope. Items from cars and so on."

"Like the last one he doesn't look like a junkie."

Vledder shook his head, a puzzled look on his face.

"You're right. It surprised me ... just like Erik Bavel."

"Why is that?"

Vledder spread wide his hands. He was looking for words.

"It's just like—like they've been transformed. They're like fresh laundry, washed, rinsed, and pressed. I hesitate to use the term born again, but something happened to them, something redeeming."

He gestured again behind him.

"I know," he continued, "these two used for years. But looking carefully at their arms, there are no recent tracks and no scars."

"They could both have changed spots," said DeKok. "Addicts shoot up almost anywhere, even between the toes."

"Perhaps," answered Vledder, "but I have a feeling that we won't find any puncture marks anywhere else, either." He paused. "No," he said, shaking his head, "these men appear clean." He paused again and then shook his head once more. "You'd almost think there's some nut going around strangling junkies who kicked the habit."

"I hope not," grimaced DeKok.

"Yes," agreed Vledder, "it reeks of bad horror movies."

DeKok bit down on his lower lip. Vledder's reasoning had interested him, but it had not warmed him. The cold of night was seeping into his bones. Chill vapors rose from the water in the canal. He shivered. He pulled up the collar of his raincoat and thought.

He looked around. All was quiet on the canal. Across the water, a few rats rustled between the parked cars. In the distance a late trolley screeched through a curve.

DeKok sighed deeply.

"Why don't you wait for the herd," he said. "I don't feel like listening to their complaints about two corpses, so close together. Weelen will be particularly upset. They probably called him just after he got home from the last one."

Vledder smiled. He knew that DeKok invariably referred to the crime scene investigators as the "Thundering Herd," an allusion to a famous Big Band. He had been prompted to make that observation because, in addition to the CSI, a number of high-ranking officers always showed up sooner or later. They did not contribute anything to the investigation, appearing solely for the PR.

"And what are you going to do?" asked Vledder.

DeKok's face became hard.

"I'm going to wish a boardinghouse keeper a good night."

With a broad grin on his face, DeKok rattled loudly on the kitchen door. He knew that there was a living room and a bedroom behind the kitchen. Those and a bathroom constituted the living quarters of the boardinghouse keeper. He dug back in his memory and remembered that years ago he had been marginally involved with the investigation of a suspicious fire on the premises. It looked like arson, but nothing could be proved. The evidence was a strange combination of a flaming saucepan near an open container of turpentine. They finally concluded the cause was carelessness.

While he waited he wondered if the same woman owned the place now. After the fire his colleagues in the criminal branch were convinced she had started the fire, possibly, to collect the insurance. The impression of wrongdoing lingered, even though the investigation was inconclusive.

He smiled wryly to himself, recalling the many petty and major crimes he had encountered in his long career as a cop. The most distasteful part was the mountain of reports he had written. A real writer would have been able to convert his experience into a series of books. At least, thanks to Vledder and his computer, he no longer struggled to produce piles of paper.

Meanwhile he drummed another series of knocks on the door. The sound rang through the staircase and landings above, echoing from the whitewashed walls.

Finally, after several minutes, the kitchen door opened cautiously. Through the crack a set of green eyes looked at him with enmity.

"Are you crazy?"

DeKok shook his head.

"No, not yet."

"Who are you?"

DeKok pushed against the door, widening the opening. He recognized the face.

"My name," he said with dignity, "is DeKok. With kay-oh-kay. In case you want to complain about me, you'll be able to spell my name correctly. I insist on that."

The woman cocked her head.

"You are police?"

DeKok nodded. He saw in her eyes that she remembered him.

"I'd like to talk to you. Not about a fire, this time, but about a young man who was found dead in your rooms. My colleague said your willingness to cooperate is lacking."

She pressed her thin lips together and shook her head.

"I want nothing to do with it," she said after a long pause.

DeKok gave her a winning smile.

"That will be difficult," he said reasonably. "You discovered the corpse under your roof."

She reacted angrily. Her nostrils flared.

"I'm not responsible for the behavior of my lodgers. They go their own way." She lifted a sharp chin. "You ever heard of privacy?"

DeKok suppressed a sharp retort regarding a coffee pot. He was not here to antagonize her. But he was faced with a set of murders. He needed immediate answers. With a friendly, but insistent gesture, he took her hand from the door handle and pushed the door farther into the kitchen.

"Mrs. Lyons," he began mildly, "eh … that is your name, isn't it?"

"You know very well."

DeKok looked around the kitchen.

"My memory of this kitchen is an unpleasant one."

She grinned with a crooked mouth.

"It was all much ado over nothing."

DeKok smiled shyly.

"But I do recall you had a cozy living room." His tone was bantering. "Why don't we continue our conversation there?"

Mrs. Lyons gave him a long, searching look. Then she suddenly gave in and led the way to the living room.

DeKok carefully closed the kitchen door and ambled after her.

In the living room he looked around. The room was relatively unchanged. The kitsch on the mantelpiece was all there. The carpet had seen better days. The chairs sported the tatty, imitation velvet upholstery he remembered.

Without being asked, DeKok took a seat and placed his little hat on the floor.

"How long has that boy been living here?"

Mrs. Lyons tightened her dressing gown and sat down in the chair across from DeKok.

DeKok knew she was close to fifty years old. She still looked good for her age. The skin of her face was a bit tawny, but her abundant hair was still a natural black. Her legs, although encased by a set of awful slippers, were still shapely.

"How long has that boy been living here?" he repeated.

"About eight months."

"Did he pay on time?"

"His mother paid his rent."

"From Heemstede?"

She nodded.

"Every month she sent a check. She gave me her phone number ... just in case."

DeKok looked at her intently.

"Have you let her know the boy is dead?"

Mrs. Lyons shook her head.

"I'm afraid." She spoke softly, almost whispering. "Between the two of us I just can't bring myself to make the call. You see, the woman already lost a son."

She paused, rested her hands in her lap. Suddenly she stood up and confronted DeKok with an angry look.

"Besides, what should I do with some whining old

bitch." It sounded cruel and biting. "I've got my own troubles."

DeKok did not answer but rubbed the bridge of his nose with a little finger. The sudden mood swing was no surprise. Women in Amsterdam's seamy inner city grew hard and embittered before they reached midlife. He gave her time to get the vitriol out of her system. He could not expect her to share any confidences otherwise. He shrugged it off.

"Why so hard, Mina." he asked mildly, after a long pause. "After all, it's her child."

"I'm not hard."

DeKok looked disapproving.

"Then why do you act like a virago?"

Her face turned red. She gesticulated with both hands.

"You ever run a boardinghouse? Do you have to fight for every penny? Always on the look-out, so they won't slip away in the dead of night without paying?" She shook her head sarcastically. "No, not you. The State cuts your check every month, right on time. All you have to do is walk to the mailbox."

DeKok gave her an apologetic look and laughed. He held up his hand with the thumb and index finger separated a short distance.

"It's just a small check. My wife complains every month she can't make it on my minuscule salary." He noticed her smile in response. "Besides," he added, "you certainly had no trouble with Erik Bavel ... I mean, financially?"

"No."

"What kind of boy was he?"

She crossed her arms and forced a shiver.

"He was a soft egg. You understand? He was the sensitive

type, so weak. I bet he was overprotected by doting parents, or a doting mama. That type always messes up, sooner or later. It's inevitable."

"Messes up, how?"

"Ach, you know what I mean. Kids who are indulged have no resistance to pressures—get hooked on drugs. When the parents catch on the money runs dry. It's a downhill ride. They start with petty crimes. But they are not suited for purse snatching, let alone real felonies. So the arrests start; with any luck they're in long enough to get clean for a while—"

DeKok interrupted.

"So, you knew he was an addict?"

She pointed at the phone on the wall.

"His mother told me. After a while he talked to me. He told me how difficult it had been, admitted there were times he resigned himself to die of an overdose." Suddenly a soft smile fled across her face, giving her a momentary look of tenderness. "Anyone would admire him for kicking the habit. He was clean and studying hard, lately."

DeKok nodded agreement.

"Do you have any idea why somebody would want to kill him?"

Mina Lyons shrugged her shoulders.

"I don't understand a thing. That's why I refused to believe he was dead, at first. When I came into his room, he seemed to be dozing off in his chair. I even yelled at him because he had been making coffee in his room." She shook her head and bit her lower lip. "I'm a bit crazy at times. I go berserk for the silliest reasons. The least little thing can set me off, for no reason at all. I didn't see he was dead, not at once."

"How did you come to realize?"

"What?"

"That he had been murdered."

She stretched her neck and pointed at her throat.

"I saw the spots on his neck. That's why I came back here and called the police. I was in a panic and angry at myself for having yelled at hi … his corpse, at him." She shook her head, as if to banish a bad memory. "Then your colleague showed up. Just another young punk who thinks he knows it all. He wanted to ask me questions. Well, I wasn't ready to talk to him, or anybody. So I threw him out."

"That wasn't very nice."

She made a dismissive gesture.

"Those young cops are always so full of themselves. I don't care for smug, self-important *boys*. They get on my nerves."

DeKok changed the subject.

"Did Erik have any enemies?"

She shook her head slowly.

"Not as far as I know, at least not as long as he's been living here. Of course, I don't know what he did while he was still hooked. Addicts are capable of anything—theft, murder, you name it." She sighed deeply. "I only knew him as a quiet, friendly young man who never bothered anybody."

"Did he still have contact with anybody in the drug scene?"

She hesitated for a moment.

"No," she said finally, "I don't think so—just Jean-Paul."

DeKok winced inwardly.

"Jean-Paul who?" he asked, tension in his voice.

"Jean-Paul Stappert, he lives upstairs. His room is next to Erik's room."

DeKok swallowed hard.

"We, eh, we ... " he hesitated. "We found Jean-Paul about an hour ago at the edge of Emperors Canal. Murdered."

Confusion filled her face.

"Murdered?" she gasped, her face ashen.

"Yes, strangled, just like Erik."

Mrs. Lyons stared at the old sleuth. It took a while for reality to hit. Then her mouth fell open and she collapsed slowly. With wide, expressionless eyes she slumped into the chair behind her.

4

Vledder pushed the keyboard of his computer aside and looked at DeKok, who was seated across from him.

"And?"

"What?"

"How was it in the lion's den?"

"You mean the living room of Mrs. Lyons?"

Vledder grinned.

"Isn't that the same thing?"

DeKok smiled briefly.

"Ach," he said, "it wasn't too bad."

Vledder winced.

"You should have heard the way she reamed me. It was quite an experience, let me tell you. I've heard some ranting, to say the least. I really believe she would have torn me a new one, had I had stayed in that kitchen one second longer."

DeKok shrugged.

"Yes," admitted DeKok, "That is classic Mina. She'll lovingly hit you in the neck with a piece of pipe. Seconds later she'll cry real tears over a ladybug with a broken wing."

"She's colorful, alright."

DeKok smiled.

"I remember her from way back when she sat in the window as a prostitute. They called her Crazy Mina, even then. On warm evenings she'd dance in Old Church

Square without panties. As she twirled her skirts lifted. On the front steps of the Old Church onlookers could see everything."

"Now that's entertainment!"

DeKok nodded.

"Yes, indeed. I admit to standing among the spectators to take in the show." The old man fell silent, steeped in memories. "She had a stone cutter among her clients. John, John Lyons was his name. He was almost twenty years older than she. He had inhaled too much marble dust and could work no longer. One day he told her he loved her. No other man had used the "L" word, except in the throws of passion. He was sincere. She left the life, and bought the rooming house with her savings. She worked like a dog from early in the morning till late at night, but the profits never amounted to much. About five years ago John Lyons died—his lungs simply gave out. Mina was hard before; now she is bitter."

For a long time both remained silent. It was Vledder who finally broke the silence.

"She tell you anything?"

"How do you mean?"

"What did she say about the murders?"

DeKok waved vaguely in the air.

"They were friends."

Vledder was surprised.

"Jean-Paul Stappert and Erik Bavel were buddies?"

DeKok nodded.

"According to Mina they were very friendly with each other."

"How friendly were they?"

Again DeKok made a vague gesture.

"Their rooms were adjoining. Because Erik's room was a bit bigger and had more light, Jean-Paul used to spend a lot of time there. Actually, he used his own room just for sleeping."

Vledder leaned forward.

"Any, eh, homosexual activity?"

DeKok rubbed his chin.

"No, I don't think so. Mina did not hint at it in any way. I didn't ask her, but as far as I know our Mina, she would have certainly told me, if there had been anything like that."

"If they were homosexual?"

"Exactly. A secret like that she would have shared immediately. She did say that she found Erik a soft, somewhat weak person."

"How candid was she?"

DeKok did not answer at once.

"She only really opened up once," he said thoughtfully. After a long pause he added, "I had barely a brush with her, professionally. It was in connection with the suspected arson, shortly after her husband died. At the time she seemed to have given up hope. She would have liked to see the entire house go up in flames. I reminded her of our encounter, and it helped. In the beginning she was still a bit reluctant, but it didn't last long. I did detect a certain amount of feeling for both young men." He paused and then added slowly: "The fainting surprised me, though."

"What?"

DeKok almost smiled.

"I asked her whether Erik Bavel still had connections in the drug world. As far as she knew he only met with Jean-Paul in the next room. When I told her we had found

Jean-Paul Stappert near Emperors Canal she collapsed into her chair." He paused. "It was a strange sight," he added.

"How do you mean?"

"She didn't try to keep her dignity intact."

"At least she wasn't acting."

DeKok shook his head

"Certainly not. It took more than a minute before she came to … not with the classic 'where am I,' but with a deep sigh and a look of recognition in her eyes."

Vledder frowned.

"Still," he commented, "it's peculiar. The murder of Erik Bavel, a murder under her own roof, hardly gets under her surface. She discovers the murder herself, but just acts annoyed. When you tell her about Stappert's murder, she is deeply affected. She can't handle it and faints dead away."

DeKok nodded agreement.

"As I said, I thought it strange as well. I told her so."

"And?"

"She said it was cumulative; she was already on overload. Said she had not been feeling well for some time. And the news about Jean-Paul engulfed her, sort of took it over the top."

Vledder snorted.

"And you believed her?"

"It sounded reasonable," nodded DeKok. "I really couldn't argue. It seemed futile to argue about her feelings, so I didn't pursue it. Still, she knew more than she was telling me. But why would she deliberately hold something back?"

He paused and rubbed the back of his little finger over the bridge of his nose. After a long pause, he resumed.

"Frankly the woman looked so distressed I felt compelled

to end the interrogation. I offered to call a doctor. She flatly refused—no surprise."

"Do you think she's somehow connected with the case?"

"With one, or both murders?" There was a tone of doubt in DeKok's voice.

"It's a possibility, isn't it?" challenged Vledder.

"It could be," answered DeKok, deep in thought, "time is the issue."

"You mean, how would she have had time to murder one or both?"

DeKok grinned without mirth.

"She would have had to get from her boardinghouse to Emperors Canal, or vice versa." He held up a finger and pointed at the clock on the wall. "There's just not enough time between the two. According to Dr. Koning it is always difficult to pinpoint the time of death, but we can be reasonably sure each man died around ten o'clock. The killer had a brief window of opportunity to strike twice. The timeframe for both killings was likely a half-hour, maybe less."

"Well," said Vledder, a mocking tone in his voice, "our strangler had quite a busy day. Two young men in such short order ..." He did not complete the sentence, looked at DeKok. "That is, if we assume one person strangled both victims."

DeKok nodded slowly.

"In view of the *modus operandi* —the almost identical marks on each victim's throat—I think we can call it a reasonable assumption, for now."

Vledder stared into the distance for a while.

"Thus," he said finally, "we are looking for a man, or a woman, who had some kind of link to both victims."

"Very good, Dick," praised DeKok.

The praise inspired Vledder.

"The motive is not related to either Stappert, or Bavel. It relates to the two, as a couple, a unit." His face became serious. "The boardinghouse owner, Mrs. Lyons, would then be our prime suspect. Or maybe," he added thoughtfully, "we need to look at the other boarders. This seems like a priority, before we investigate further."

DeKok did not react. He had heard Vledder. Aside from DeKok's usual skepticism, doubt was eating away at him. He convinced himself the answer was subtle. The reality of these crimes was somehow convoluted. He couldn't quite get to the missing elements.

Fatigue set in. DeKok tried to shake it off, rubbing his eyes. It had been a late night, the night before. It was too late to hope for a normal night's sleep. When he finally found his bed, he was unable to fall asleep. His thoughts persisted, swirling in his mind. He had so many questions and not enough answers. No answers, as a matter of fact. Once his mind became clouded and lethargic he still couldn't physically relax. Finally he arose and took a cold shower. Exhaustion won and his mind remained as slow and listless as his body.

Even now, he was still in a sort of stupor. He had trouble concentrating—wished he could just sink back in his chair and fall asleep and dream. How he longed to be in a harmonious dream world, populated by peaceful, happy people.

Vledder interrupted his escape.

"Do we have a list of names from the boardinghouse?"

DeKok looked at him through half-closed eyes.

"What?"

Vledder made an impatient gesture.

"With the personal information on Mrs. Lyons' boarders, we can screen them for criminal records."

"Well," said DeKok, irked, "can't you start with the data you have and your computer? I don't have the names or anything. You were taking everything down in your notebook."

"Of course," said Vledder, sheepishly, "I just …"

He halted. There was a loud banging on the door to the detective room. Through the frosted glass they could see the outline of a person in some sort of wide cape.

"Come in," yelled Vledder across the nearly deserted room.

It took a while before the door finally opened slowly. A heavy set man appeared in the door opening. With a theatrical gesture he swung his cape over one shoulder and approached at a slow pace, a slight smile on his face.

DeKok noticed the slow pace, the perceptible hesitation of the left leg. Slowly his gaze traveled upward to the face. He estimated the man to be in his late forties. He had a round, fleshy face with red, broken veins under the skin of the cheeks, flanking a wide, full moustache. Long, graying hair came down in waves to his shoulders.

DeKok closed his eyes momentarily, as if to call up a mental picture. Something about the man was familiar. He had seen the visitor somewhere, but could not place him, not yet. While he searched his memory, he stood up and pushed a chair closer to the desk. With a polite gesture he invited the man to sit down.

"My name is DeKok," he said in a friendly tone of voice,

"DeKok with kay-oh-kay." He pointed at Vledder. "And this is Vledder, my partner, and hope for the future."

The visitor smiled and unhooked his cape.

"My name is Alex Waardenburg." He paused, as if for effect. "Do you know me?"

DeKok reseated himself and shook his head.

"You seem familiar," he said hesitatingly. "I have, I think, seen you somewhere, but ..."

Waardenburg waved the rest of the sentence away.

"For years now," he said, in a pleasant base voice, "I've been the second violinist of the Municipal Symphonic Orchestra. Since we give a number of performances on television, lots of people see my face. Some have that sense of recognition." He added, trying too hard to appear nonchalant, "That's why I asked, you see."

DeKok smiled politely.

"How may we be of service?"

Alex Waardenburg raised his left hand in a gesture as if he were gripping the neck of a violin.

"I'm not just the second fiddle of the orchestra," he said, "I'm also a musical pedagogue."

DeKok smiled, Mostly, with his eyes.

"You're a music teacher?"

Mr. Waardenburg pursed his lips.

"Music teacher." He seemed to taste the word on his tongue. "It sounds banal, almost vulgar. Besides teaching is not my primary or my secondary living. The income, such as it is, means nothing. Fortunately, I'm financially independent." He let out a jolly laugh. "My great-grandfather had a knack for market timing; he made a fortune buying and selling stocks." His tone changed again. "I help young people along ... strictly for my own satisfaction. I get a great deal of satisfaction watching amateurs develop and mature in their musical ambitions. Yes," he repeated, "I derive a great deal of pleasure from my contributions."

DeKok nodded.

"I can understand that. Talent is rare, and promising musicians deserve nurturing. He paused for a moment and looked sharply at Waardenburg, "Surely you didn't come here to discuss the merits of advancing musical careers."

The visitor's face fell.

"I ... eh, ... I heard," he began softly, "you found a body on Emperor's Canal. It was near my house."

"That is the location, right."

Waardenburg swallowed hard.

"I came to ask if whether you need me to view the remains. I think I can identify the victim."

DeKok narrowed his eyes.

"What makes you think so?"

Waardenburg hesitated for a moment.

"It's all a bit confusing. Perhaps I should tell you from the beginning."

DeKok nodded thoughtfully.

"Please continue, if you wish."

Waardenburg settled in his chair.

"About a year ago a young man came to my house and asked me to teach him. He was different from the usual type of young person who approaches me. He was poorly dressed, unkempt, and much older. He was thin. He appeared to be about twenty-five years old. Frankly I did not feel inclined to take him on. Although I accept a few older students, if one wants to get anywhere in the music world, one must begin very young. Besides this fellow did not play a single instrument. He could not read, nor write, music. In fact he seemed a hopeless case and—"

DeKok interrupted.

"But you did take him on as a student?"

The visitor nodded.

"I've wondered about that myself. He was so enthusiastic and determined to learn. It became very apparent, even during that first interview. It was a wonder to behold how he literally absorbed anything to do with music … it was as if he had thirsted for many years and finally had an opportunity to drink his fill."

"And he made progress?"

"Certainly. He really started to get the hang of writing music, reading it, too."

"How often did you work with him?"

"Daily, except on the weekends and when I performed with the orchestra."

"Did you have a fixed appointment?"

"He always came for lessons at night, from ten to eleven. Sometimes we ran over for a half hour, or so."

DeKok nodded his understanding.

"Did you have a performance last night?"

"No."

"So, he should have been there at ten o'clock last night?"

"Yes."

DeKok gave him a searching look.

"But he didn't show?"

"No."

"Didn't you think that was strange?"

The musical pedagogue shook his head.

"It is infrequent, but students have failed to show without an explanation."

DeKok's face became a steel mask. He leaned forward.

"But Mr. Stappert wasn't the type to skip a lesson, Mr. Waardenburg." His voice was severe, almost accusing. "Jean-Paul Stappert wouldn't willingly miss a thing. Not a minute. How did you put that again? Oh yes: 'It was a wonder to behold how he literally absorbed anything to do with music … it was as if he had thirsted for many years and finally had an opportunity to drink his fill.'"

Alex Waardenburg spread two mighty arms in a gesture of surrender.

"Jean-Paul," he cried out dramatically, "is twenty-five years old. He's an adult with his own life. He had the strength of character to fight his way out of drug addiction. Should I be worried, or find it strange, that a man like that doesn't show up for a music lesson?"

DeKok gave him a long, searching look.

"How close were you to him?"

"I don't know what you mean by that question?"

"Are you homosexual?"

"I have a wife and a twenty-seven year old son."

"That doesn't answer my question. Did you or did you not have a homosexual relationship with Jean-Paul?"

"No … I was his music teacher … that's all."

"Did Jean-Paul ever miss a lesson before last night?"

"No."

"And yet, when he failed to show, you didn't find it odd?"

Alex Waardenburg jumped up from his chair.

"I didn't think it odd," he yelled. "There was nothing strange about it." He paused, dropped his chin and sighed. "But I felt fear."

"Why?"

"I was afraid something had happened to him."

"Why?"

Waardenburg sat down again and covered his face with his hands. He did not say anything.

DeKok leaned closer.

"Why were you afraid something might have happened to him?"

The man took his hands away from his face.

"Jean-Paul," he said softly, "was a special young man. I have never before encountered such a personality. He had a certain aura about him. Sometimes I would catch myself answering questions he had not yet asked, but that he had already formed in his mind. It's difficult to explain, but it was a strange experience. Sometimes I knew what he thought without a word passing between us." He sighed deeply. "Last night I thought that Jean-Paul was approaching his own death."

DeKok swallowed.

"And you did nothing?"

Alex Waardenburg closed both eyes tightly. Clearly the old sleuth's question tormented him.

"What could I have done?" It was a cry of despair. "There was nothing concrete, but I sensed his fear."

"He was afraid of death?"

"Yes."

"And he was on his way to your place?"

Alex Waardenburg looked dumbfounded and bewildered.

"It wasn't me. No. It wasn't me. I had nothing to do with his death."

"Did anyone imply you were involved in any way?"

The man grinned sheepishly.

"You ... eh, you could think that ... because ... because Jean-Paul was found dead so close to my house and I sensed his death." He grinned vacantly. A stupefied look took over his intelligent face. "But," he continued, "it was all coincidence, logistics. Death obeys its own laws." He spread two shaking hands in front of him and stared at them intently. "Jean-Paul," he whispered, "had no reason to be afraid of me, or my house. On the contrary I felt nothing in my heart but friendship and admiration for him."

DeKok scratched the back of his neck. He was a bit at a loss with the eccentric musician. He alternated between self-accusatory and vague. DeKok and Vledder knew people falsely confessed (some, regularly) to attract attention. After his ramblings he leaned back in his chair.

"When did you know Jean-Paul was dead?"

Waardenburg pressed his hands against his temples.

"After ten o'clock," he said thoughtfully, "after ten o'clock I no longer felt his presence. That worried me ... it worried me more then when I still felt something."

"But you stayed at home?"

"By quarter past ten Jean-Paul had not shown up, I left the house to go looking for him."

"Where did you go?"

"I headed for his rooming house on Prince Henry Quay."

With a sudden movement DeKok pressed himself upright in his chair.

"And?"

Alex Waardenburg shook his head. His eyes were big and his face was ashen.

"Jean-Paul wasn't there. There was another dead young man in his chair."

5

_____

After Alex Waardenburg had left, Vledder jumped up from his chair. There were red spots on his cheeks. With a wild gesture he threw both arms up in the air.

"Nonsense," he yelled agitatedly, "pure nonsense."

DeKok, absent-mindedly, looked up.

"What?"

Vledder came closer to the desk.

"He kept on yakking about impulses, auras. It was pure New Age mumbo jumbo. How could Jean-Paul know he was about to die? How could he possibly know some weirdo was planning to strangle him? If that wasn't strange enough the crackpot 'felt' Jean-Paul knew his death was imminent. What sort of connection is he imagining? Other than a radio or cell phone—what?"

Vledder sounded exasperated, as well as mocking. DeKok laughed.

"They must have had something."

Vledder got excited all over again.

"I sat there listening and I couldn't believe my ears."

"Why is that?"

Vledder gesticulated wildly.

"You swallowed it whole! You treated him like a believable witness." He pulled a chair nearby and straddled it backward. "Do you remember what we're investigating,

DeKok? Do you? We are supposed to be investigating the facts surrounding a straightforward murder—two murders. This double murder will be solved by old-fashioned police work and forensic applications. What we have here is some abstract, nebulous mess about people who feel people feeling death overtake them."

DeKok smiled.

"You may be judging me too hastily. We have solved worse than this. No matter what, I'll never set aside the importance of classical investigative techniques. But, tell me, what should I have done? Should I have told Waardenburg right from the start not to burden me with his nonsense? That would be an arrogant approach. We need to know how he thinks. In addition, I managed to pluck out some useful tidbits of information."

Vledder sighed.

"Sorry. It was torment listening to the two of you. I kept squelching an almost irresistible impulse to interrupt."

DeKok winked slowly.

"I'm glad you decided not to interrupt. Had you broken in he might have been less candid. From any angle Alex Waardenburg is plenty strange. That said I believe he had a particularly close relationship with Jean-Paul Stappert. Remember when he said sometimes he 'would catch himself answering questions his student had not yet asked?' Whether or not we accept it as truth, it has an eerie quality."

"More so, if true," scoffed Vledder.

DeKok ignored the remark.

"But there were other remarkable parts to his story. When Jean-Paul had not shown up by quarter past ten, the feelings, or lack of them, drove Waardenburg to the rooming house. There he found the corpse of Erik Bavel."

DeKok raised an index finger into the air. "That's what Waardenburg told us ... what he wants us to believe."

Vledder looked nonplussed.

"But he came here of his own accord. We didn't summon him."

DeKok changed the direction of his index finger and pointed it at Vledder.

"Here's the challenge. You don't believe in impulses, auras, or telepathy. Well, if it was not one of these, why would Waardenburg go to the rooming house? Was he worried about Jean-Paul's absence, or did he have other motives?"

Vledder nodded agreement.

"Other motives," he said decisively.

"All right ... what motives?"

Vledder shrugged.

"That remains to be seen as the investigation goes forward. In any case, he knew exactly where Jean-Paul lived. It would be a good idea to find out if he's been to that rooming house before." He paused for effect. "You understand, DeKok," he continued, "based on Waardenburg's statements he did not only know Jean-Paul; he must have known Erik Bavel, as well."

DeKok looked thoughtfully at his young colleague.

"If your theory is correct the murderer had some sort of relationship with both victims. In that case Alex Waardenburg becomes our prime suspect."

Vledder smiled.

"You'll see! I'm right this time."

DeKok gave him an admiring look.

"It's about time." He changed his tone. "I'll say this for you, sometimes you have glimmers of real intelligence."

The young inspector stood up and uttered some barely audible grunts. DeKok laughed heartily. Sometimes he felt like stimulating the thinking process of his former student with a bit of derision. It was never malicious, never insulting. He felt too strong a bond with his long-time partner for that. They had solved numerous cases together, sometimes in dangerous situations. A bond had grown between him and Vledder, which was stronger than the usual partnership between cops.

DeKok's phone rang. He reached for it, but Vledder had already picked it up. Vledder listened in silence. After a few seconds he covered the mouth piece. He looked at DeKok.

"Mrs. Bavel is downstairs. According to the desk sergeant, she knows all about her son's death. She wants to talk to you."

DeKok nodded.

"Send her up."

DeKok approached her slowly, almost languidly, with drooping shoulders. His head was bent to one side and there was a sad expression on his face. His demeanor was a symbol, an expression of sorrow and understanding. It was genuine, not a practiced act for the occasion. He felt real empathy with the grieving woman. Hesitatingly he took her hand.

"Please accept my condolences," he said gravely, "for the loss of your son, Erik."

He led her to the chair next to his desk.

"As I understand it, you suffered another loss, not too long ago."

Mrs. Bavel bowed her head.

"Yes, my son Ricky ... a year and a half ago ... killed by drugs." She sighed deeply. "I was so happy when everything started to go so well for Erik. He stopped using and he was studying hard, partly with the support of Jean-Paul. He seemed to have lit a spark in Erik."

"You're talking about Jean-Paul Stappert?"

Her lip quivered.

"That boy ... that boy ... they killed him, too. It's just barbaric, bestial."

DeKok sat down behind his desk. He would have liked to tell her that she was being unfair to animals, but he controlled himself. He understood her feelings and in his heart he agreed with her. He leaned backward in his chair and studied her face. She looked to be around fifty years old, maybe a little younger. She was slender and had a beautiful, oval face with dark, almond-shaped eyes. The eyes were filled with tears.

"You've already visited the rooming house?"

Mrs. Bavel lowered her head.

"Yes, Mrs. Lyons called me on the phone early this morning. She told me she had been unable to sleep all night, and couldn't get up the courage to tell me what had happened." She fell silent, opened the handbag on her lap, and took a tidy little handkerchief from it. Carefully she dried her eyes. "Mrs. Lyons," she went on, "has been a big help, a support, the last few months. She kept me informed about what was happening ... with Erik."

DeKok nodded his understanding.

"Did she talk to you about Jean-Paul? I mean, about his death?"

Mrs. Bavel nodded.

"What gets into people? Why kill these two boys?"

There was both anger and resignation in her voice. "What is the sense of it?"

"You think the same person killed both boys?" DeKok asked.

Mrs. Bavel looked surprised.

"Isn't that obvious? They've both been strangled."

DeKok decided to change the subject.

"You had a good relationship with Erik?"

"Of course, why would you ask?"

"I mean, you didn't just stay in touch through telephone contact with Mina Lyons?"

Mrs. Bavel shook her head.

"Erik came often to Heemstede, especially since Ricky's death. We developed a real bond, stronger than ever before. I am sure Erik kicked his drug habit because of me. I kept reminding him I didn't want to loose two sons in such a meaningless way." More tears welled in her eyes. "Now he's dead, anyway." Her face became harder. Her mouth set in a determined expression and she swallowed. She aimed a penetrating look at DeKok. Hate burned through the tears in her eyes.

"You *will* find him, won't you? You *must* find him ... the murderer. You hear!? You must find him!"

DeKok rubbed his face. The sudden change of demeanor and tone confused him a bit.

"I ... eh, I will do my best." It sounded like a precautionary excuse. "Of course," he continued, hesitatingly, "there are no guarantees."

Her face became softer, milder.

"I understand." Her tone was more reasonable, more understanding. "I spoke out of anger. This is infuriating, so senseless, so ... incomprehensible. It is enraging to a parent.

I can't help dwelling on what was going on in the mind of that killer, that animal."

DeKok gave her a wan smile.

"That's only known to the murderer ... and to God."

Mrs. Bavel stared into the distance. She did not react. She seemed to have forgotten her surroundings. The concept of God did not interest her. DeKok pulled his chair closer and leaned forward.

"Are you the only one who grieves for your sons? I mean, are you married, where is the father?"

A sad smile formed around her lips.

"My husband never cared much for Erik or Ricky, not even when they were young. His disappointment always showed. He devoted his love exclusively to his eldest son, Ramon. Ramon is the strongest of his boys. He's a lot like my husband, steady, domineering, willful. Erik and Ricky were more like me ... softer, more sensitive." She shrugged her shoulders. "And more easily hurt."

DeKok nodded.

"And that's why they became addicted."

It sounded harder then he intended.

Mrs. Bavel looked at the gray sleuth with condemnation in her eyes.

"If you mean, were they spoiled or weak, they were not! Ricky fought long and hard against his addiction. There were periods when he hardly used at all. His struggle ended tragically ... like so many. Deep down I think the overdose could have been intentional. He could have seen suicide as a final escape from misery." She paused. Then she added: "Erik didn't loose hope—he stayed the course long enough to get free and stay that way."

Instinctively DeKok felt he had gone too far.

"I didn't mean to cast aspersions on your sons," he said apologetically. "I don't have the right to do that. I never knew them and don't know the circumstances leading to their addiction. Young people often have problems, difficulties, that—"

Mrs. Bavel interrupted. Her eyes spat fire and she screamed.

"But I *know*," she cried. She slammed both hands on the desk. She looked like a trapped animal. "Their brother, Ramon, got them hooked. He's the one who poisoned my two sons, and he did it on purpose. He supplied them with their first heroin ... as a test."

DeKok's look of astonishment encouraged her to go on.

"Test?" asked Vledder, but DeKok waved him to silence as he held Mrs. Bavel with his eyes.

She nodded vaguely in Vledder's direction and refocused on DeKok.

"Yes, he made a pact with Erik and Ricky. We never knew until it was too late. They were going to use heroin every day for a week. After a week it would be obvious which one was the strongest—he would be the one who wouldn't need it anymore. It was a dare between very competitive kids."

DeKok closed his eyes. Slowly he processed the amazing information.

"Incredible," he said after a long pause. "Why would anybody propose such a test?"

Mrs. Bavel sighed deeply.

"Ramon passed the test with flying colors. He wasn't totally focused on his own agenda, even as a child."

DeKok swallowed.

"But Ricky and Erik became hopelessly addicted."

She nodded to herself, again drying her eyes with her handkerchief.

"Ramon gloated openly. He never made a secret of it. On the day Ricky died, he and his friends had a party. He called it a victory celebration." Suddenly she stopped and stared at DeKok with frightened eyes. It seemed as if a terrible thought had formed in her head.

"Ramon," she took a deep breath. Then, still looking scared, she went on, "Ramon almost choked with anger and disappointment when the family talked about Erik's success … about how he was staying clean and sober. It went beyond resenting a sibling—he was furious. He acted as though his brother had betrayed him."

6

Vledder stared at DeKok with a look of total disbelief.

"That, eh, is not a human response. Ramon's behavior was demonic. It takes a sick, a very sick, brain to hatch a scheme to gain superiority over your siblings by destroying their lives."

DeKok stared at Vledder without seeing him. He too, found it difficult to accept the concept. He needed time to absorb it. It was simply too bizarre.

"We'll have to talk to this Ramon," he said after a long pause.

Vledder was confused.

"Ramon? Why? He cannot be prosecuted for making addicts out of his brothers. We'd have to pick up every user in the country. They will all have tried to get friends or acquaintances to start using. Sometimes it's co-dependents they want. Sometimes they need to bring new customers to their dealers."

DeKok shook his head.

"That's not what I meant at all. I want to check his alibi for the time of the murders."

"Not really?"

"Yes, is that so strange?"

Vledder swallowed and then spoke the obvious.

"You suspect he may be responsible for both murders, that he's our strangler."

DeKok nodded emphatically.

"The Bavels of Heemstede are wealthy people. Let's assume Ramon, the eldest, doesn't want to share the eventual inheritance. His mother characterizes him as having always had an agenda. He had a perfect motive, don't you think?" He waved in Vledder's direction. "Ramon is not only ruthless, he is clever. He thinks up a dare testing their ability to withstand the addiction and it works better than he hopes. Brother Ricky is soon no longer a player ... reason for a party, a victory celebration. Erik seems well on the way to his demise ... icing on the cake."

Vledder interrupted.

"But Erik kicked the habit, cleaned up his act and was able to continue his studies."

DeKok grinned malevolently.

"You see, that was a miscalculation. Hence Ramon's anger. How did his mother put it: 'He almost choked with anger and disappointment.' A means of manipulating his brother, Erik, seems pretty well impossible. There's only one way out—"

Vledder interrupted again.

"Murder," he sighed.

DeKok raised a finger in the air.

"And who helped Erik kick the habit ... who offered him moral support? That would be the man who spoiled Ramon's plans."

"Jean-Paul Stappert."

DeKok fell back in his chair.

"Et voilà ... we have our motive and our murderer."

For just a moment Vledder seemed stunned. Then he shook his head.

"I have serious doubts," he exclaimed angrily. "It's a slippery slope. Nobody is that ruthless. It is so inhuman, so calculated. You must be criminally insane to conceive of such a plan. As I said, it's just too demonic."

DeKok shrugged his shoulders.

"The question remains, exactly *how* evil is Ramon Bavel?"

It was busy in the Quarter. During holidays and vacation time tourists came from near and far. "Come and see the Red Light District of Amsterdam." The trade ran into hundreds of millions of dollars. Crowds jostled for position in front of the sex shops, stared at inflatable women surrounded by a forest of dildoes. Fragments of music floated from the bars and a thousand fragrances came from the restaurants. A couple of drunken sailors embraced each other in the middle of the street, each struggling to keep the other from falling down.

DeKok pushed his dilapidated little hat farther back on his head and shrilly whistled a Christmas carol.

Vledder, next to him, had a deep frown on his face. The speculation regarding Ramon Bavel still reverberated in his head. He couldn't shake it.

At the corner of the Old Church Square a group of wise guys and some of their women had gathered. Their gathering had an air of conspiracy. The news of the two stranglings had spread through the Quarter. The group fell silent as the two inspectors approached.

DeKok unbuttoned the top button of his shirt and pulled down his tie. It was hot in the old city. The heat of the day still clung to the old facades. The water in the canals evaporated, creating a low hanging fog around the quays and around the bridges.

The heart of the district, the so-called Walletjes, was at peak capacity. Business was brisque. Exotic girls from the Far and Near East, especially, found plenty of customers. The customers leaned against trees and walls, each waiting for a turn. As soon as a curtain opened and a customer left, another would enter the room. The curtain would be closed and the girl would ply her trade. So it has gone for ages.

DeKok observed it all philosophically. He knew the district like nobody else. He also knew the business of the Quarter had been going on for hundreds of years and would probably continue for hundreds more. Near a corner of Barns Alley he entered a bar. Vledder followed.

Lowee, generally known as "Little Lowee" throughout the Quarter, greeted his guests with enthusiastic joviality.

"Long time, no see," exclaimed the diminutive barkeeper. His mousy little face shone with pleasure and goodwill. He considered DeKok his special friend. It was a friendship that DeKok sometimes shamelessly pushed to the limits.

"I sorta thought you guys had amnesia—forgot all about me," continued Lowee. "I almost was gonna ask about youse at the barn. Maybe youse lost your compass."

DeKok had to laugh. He closed his eyes for a moment.

"No," he said, "I'll always know how to find your place. Even with my eyes closed, I'd just follow the aroma of that special cognac you keep."

Lowee smiled and watched as Vledder and DeKok hoisted themselves on the bar stools.

"And here you be," exclaimed the barkeeper, holding up a venerable bottle of cognac. It was an unknown label to Vledder and DeKok, but Lowee assured them that it could compare favorably with any of the better-known brands.

The bottle looked old and dusty and after Lowee broke the seal and removed the stopper, the aroma seemed to spread from the bottle.

With a routine gesture Lowee lined up three large cognac glasses and with bated breath they watched him pour. With silent reverence they contemplated the three filled glasses for a moment. Then DeKok lifted his glass and rocked it slightly while he held it under his nose. A blissful look appeared on his face.

"If it only taste half as good as it smells," he said. Carefully he took a sip. The other two watched him intently.

DeKok held the liquid in his mouth and then slowly swallowed it. He looked at the glass, held it up against the light.

"Lowee," he said finally, "this is an embarrassment of riches, a drink worthy of the gods."

With a happy grin, Lowee lifted his own glass and Vledder followed suit.

"And here's hoping you gonna enjoy for a long time," said Lowee.

"Amen," said Vledder.

For a long time they basked in silence.

When DeKok finally put his empty glass back on the counter, he sighed.

"You know, Lowee," he said thoughtfully, "if people would take more time out to enjoy a really great glass of cognac from time to time, maybe they would hate less, be less greedy, and would be less murderous."

The small barkeeper stared at him, the bottle in his hand for a refill.

"A beautiful thought," he said dreamily, "yeah, a nice senniment."

DeKok stared at his empty glass.

"I'm saddled with two murders. That's why—"

"I knows," answered Lowee, nodding in sympathy. "I gotta ear full 'bout dem two guys from Aunt Mina." Lowee followed the practice of the Quarter where all long-time residents were, sooner or later, referred to as "Aunt" or "Uncle."

"Yes," DeKok sighed.

"There's all kinda buzz," volunteered Lowee.

DeKok gave a questioning look.

"Talk?"

"Yeah, rumors on the street."

"What sort of rumors?"

"They says it's da mafia thassa behind it."

"Mafia? What kind of mafia. We don't have any mafia in Holland."

Lowee pointed a thumb over his shoulder and winked.

"Da dope mafia, dem big guys. Dem that control the supplies—coke, Big H."

DeKok looked pensive.

"These guys were clean, so, what would traffickers have to do with the murders?"

Little Lowee shrugged his shoulders in an apologetic gesture.

"I just tell whadda whispers is," he almost stammered. "Word on da street is dem guys was knocked off because they wasn't using."

"What?"

Lowee nodded his head emphatically.

"Dem killings is a sorta warnings, to make sure dem other junks don't do quit. Da dope mafia don't likes to loose customers, you see."

DeKok looked angry.

"That's the purest tripe. With all the money they make, why kill two ex-users as an example of ..." He did not finish the sentence. "Who has been spreading this nonsense?"

Little Lowee grinned.

"That I dunno," he answered. "Somebody tole me. I also knows there's a couple help groups inna panic."

"Help groups? What are you talking about?"

"You knows, Salvation Army and some more of dem do-gooders that wanna help da people get clean and sober."

"But why would they be in a panic?"

"They done heard, of course, what happens to dem guys. They're gettin' afraid nobody will come for help, no more."

DeKok shook his head in resignation. He knew how devastating results of such rumors can be. On the street, particularly, among the addicts, it would gain strength with every repetition. As long as people believed it and repeated it, the message would become the truth.

He paused before his next question. It was a matter of nailing the real perpetrator of the killings as soon as possible. Only that way would the rumors be stilled. He looked at Little Lowee.

"Did you know those two boys?"

"Yep."

"Both?"

Lowee shrugged his narrow shoulders.

"They come in some time. But I never got close to da one from Heemstede. Too rich for me. He was sorta quiet like, anyway. I took more to da udder one. Jean-Paul. He wassa fun guy, cheerful like, you knows. I usta call 'im Mister Melody."

"Why Mister Melody?"

"Well, Jean-Paul had a head full of tunes, you knows. Not dem poplar hits, or anything you heard before. Nossir. Brand new music ... nice music. Coulda been poplar."

"So, what did he do with the music?"

Lowee spread his hands.

"Nuthin, just nuthin. He just haddem in his head, you knows. He was real musical too, you knows. Was long time I seen a talent show where this guy moves his hand over half empty glasses and makes music. So, one day, I set up a row of beer glasses for Jean-Paul."

"And?"

There was sincere admiration on Lowee's face.

"He tries a few times. Fills some of them glasses, pours out a little of another, and then he starts to play. A wonnerful melody." He hesitated a moment. "Dint take him longer than ten minutes."

DeKok smiled.

"Perhaps he should have gone to amateur night, too."

Little Lowee nodded his head.

"Not even—the stage, whatever. I tole him so. I got some contacts by da artists. But Jean-Paul dint feel like it. He just wanna get rid of them melodies in his head. That's all."

"Did they bother him?"

"Whadda ye mean?"

"Physically, or mentally. Did they cause headaches, migraines. Did they make him sad or depressed?"

Lowee shook his head.

"Nossir. It was the friend usta be real down. But I never notice Jean-Paul. He was real cheerful when he was here, anyways." He paused, then added: "He usta say he be awake nights. He wake up, you knows, but couldn't a slept again. Dem melodies just kept him awake."

DeKok nodded slowly.

"What a shame. That boy should have found someone to help him develop his gifts."

Little Lowee poured again. Thoughtfully they sipped.

"I set him up with Willy Haarveld," said Lowee casually. "He's in da business, so to speak. Manages an orchestra and gotta bunch of singers onna contract. He's gotta group, too."

DeKok frowned.

"Willy Haarveld ... wasn't he involved in some scandal, not too long ago?"

Lowee nodded.

"Somebody tried to pop him, ambushed him."

"Where was that?"

The small barkeeper waved vaguely.

"Near his house in Laren," he grinned. "And that ain't da first time somebody tried to whack 'im. He's not always whadda you call legit. If you ain't kosher you runs risks."

"And you set up a meeting between that boy and a man like that?" censored DeKok.

Little Lowee looked offended.

"Where else *I'm* gonna send 'im?"

From Rear Fort Canal they crossed through Old Acquaintance Alley to Front Fort Canal. It was more back street. Here and there a prostitute leaned against her door. Most looked listless. The stream of clients had thinned considerably.

Vledder glanced aside.

"Do you completely reject the theory of gang intimidation?"

DeKok nodded.

"I dismissed it."

"Why not?" Drug kingpins order tortures, rapes, and executions all the time.

"Sure, if it nets results."

"Look, it makes sense. Maybe the results they wanted are the rumors we know have taken hold in the neighborhoods."

"That's exactly why it does *not* make sense," DeKok slowed down and turned toward Vledder. "Why would big dealers risk these two murders? Barely four percent of all users manage to kick the habit permanently. It makes more sense to develop aggressive distribution plans, among the schools, for instance. That way their clientele increases exponentially, more than offsetting their losses without the risk. Sure they aren't bothered by brutality, but most are smart businessmen."

Vledder grinned.

"Sounds like you're connected."

Eventually they reached Warmoes Street and entered the old station house.

Meindert Post, the tall Urker watch commander, waved them closer to the barrier.

"Mina Lyons has been here," he roared in his quarterdeck voice. "She wants you to come over as soon as possible."

DeKok lifted an eyebrow, waiting for clarification.

"What's up?" asked Vledder.

Post glanced at his notes.

"Somebody ransacked the rooms of those two boys that were killed. They even tore up the pillows and the mattresses."

7

Mrs. Lyons, the tawny rooming house keeper, pointed sadly around her.

"Just look," she whined, "it's horrible. Look at the mess. Hundreds of guilders in damage." She looked at DeKok, "Who's going to pay for that?"

DeKok ignored the question. The police did not have the funds for that kind of thing.

"Did you see them?"

"Who?"

"The men who did this, of course," he said impatiently.

Mrs. Lyons nodded vigorously, wiping the tears from her eyes.

"Yes, they came to the kitchen door. Two men. They told me they'd heard I had rooms to let and they were interested ... if the rooms were to their liking."

"Then what?"

"I showed them the rooms."

"Those were the rooms rented by Bavel and Stappert?"

The boardinghouse keeper looked surprised.

"Of course, they were available."

"Mina, their belongings were still in the rooms! And what about the police tape? Did you ignore that as well?"

Mrs. Lyons pressed her lips together in a tight line.

"You can't expect me to keep rooms vacant until the family finally gets around to removing their stuff."

DeKok did not like that answer. He gave her a hard look.

"They hardly had the time, besides, the rent is paid until the end of the month, correct?"

She snorted.

"If they don't show up today, I'll throw their stuff in the street."

DeKok sighed. He knew Mina well. There was no use arguing with her when she was ranting. With a tired gesture he pointed at the mutilated mattresses.

"Did that happen while you were here?"

Mina Lyons shook her head. Red spots of anger appeared on her cheeks.

"I would have ripped their throats out," she screamed. "No, the phone rang and I had to answer it. I left them alone—just a few minutes. When I came back, I found this."

"Where are your guests now?"

"They're out of here."

DeKok nodded to himself.

"Did you ever see them before? Were they locals?"

"No."

"Would you recognize them, if you saw them again?"

The landlady stared at the mess.

"One of them, for sure," she said after a brief hesitation. "He was tall and gaunt, with a narrow face. I'd recognize him out of thousands. He got his accent in The Hague. He did the talking. The other one just looked around, a real sneaky sort of guy."

"What ages?"

"Late twenties."

DeKok rubbed his chin, a pensive look on his face.

"You have any idea what they might have been looking for?"

Mrs. Lyons nodded at the empty cupboards, the destroyed books, the rolled-up carpet.

"Heroin, what else?"

Vledder and DeKok walked along Prince Henry Quay, past old Saint Nicholas Church. The church had seen better days. It was near Central Station.

To their left, farther along the Seadike, they saw groups of drug dealers. Bored, silent men, loitered in small groups. The plywood covered windows behind them made an ominous backdrop. The men blended into the decaying facade, carrying death with them. Every once in a while they called out to each other in raw tones.

The two inspectors passed the intersection in silence. Through St. Olof Alley they returned to Warmoes Street.

Vledder was the one to break the silence.

"Do you really think they were looking for heroin?"

DeKok shrugged.

"For Mina it's a reasonable assumption. As addicts, our two boys must have done some dealing as well. That's almost a given. It's not unlikely they had a few grams, maybe even more, hidden somewhere. Someone, maybe previous customers, would have known about a stash."

"The buzzards gathered after they died?"

"Exactly."

Vledder shook his head. His face showed irritation.

"Do you really believe that?"

"Not completely. I have some reservations. Someone

who has finally kicked the habit would want to get all the way away from the drugs and the culture." DeKok grinned sardonically. "After all a reformed alcoholic doesn't keep liquor around."

Vledder chewed his lower lip.

"So, there was nothing to score."

"No."

The younger inspector threw up his hands in a gesture of bewilderment.

"Okay, so what were they looking for?"

DeKok gave his colleague a measured look.

"If we knew that, Dick Vledder, we'd be a lot closer to a solution.

It was strangely quiet in the lobby of the station house. DeKok glanced at the clock on the wall. It was nearly one thirty in the morning. Until recently the lobby had an almost cozy atmosphere around this time. Uncle Jacob used to visit around that time. He'd sit on the bench against the wall, playing one tune after another on a battered accordion, until he fell asleep over his instrument. With his long gray hair, moustache, and beard he looked distinguished, even in his sleep. The watch commander waked him gently toward dawn and offered him a mug of coffee. Uncle Jacob would slurp the coffee and, then, disappear with his accordion into the breaking day. Nobody ever knew where he went.

A few weeks ago he did not appear. A prostitute came, instead, to report that there was an old man in the middle of the pavement in Cow Street.

The watch commander sent out two constables to have

a look. They found Uncle Jacob, soaking wet and dead. They found his accordion a few meters down the road in the portico of a store.

When the morgue attendants lifted the body on the stretcher, one of the constables folded the old man's hands on his chest. The cop gently placed the accordion at Jacob's feet.

The next morning DeKok learned about the incident. A few days later DeKok and the watch commander stood at his grave and learned for the first time that Uncle Jacob's real name was actually Petrus Sogeler.

DeKok recalled it now with nostalgia. He had met and known a great many unique characters in his long career. He had loved most of them.

He glanced at the desk. Warmoes Street Station was still laid out in the old fashioned way. It was like an old movie set. The lobby was divided by a railing, a barrier that split the space in two halves. In the center of the railing was a slightly elevated desk behind which the watch commander held his post. In the United States he would be a desk sergeant, reflected DeKok. To one side of the desk was a door that allowed officers and other authorized persons into the rest of the station. Comfortable benches and a coffee machine covered the walls in the public part of the space.

DeKok mused how different Warmoes Street was from modern station houses. They usually had more like a foyer, cramped, narrow lobby. The police were separated from the public by bullet-proof Plexiglas, with small openings to make conversation possible between the people on either side of the barrier. They were designed like some banks. In many station houses a citizen could never penetrate unhindered all the way to the bullet-proof glass. The front doors opened electronically. Visitors had to prove they needed to enter by speaking into an impersonal loudspeaker mounted in the outside wall.

DeKok thoroughly disapproved. Like a church, a police station should be accessible to all. It was not just a traffic hub for law enforcement. It was, above all, a refuge for people seeking help.

DeKok looked at the watch commander. Meindert Post had been replaced by Jan Kuster, a solid, amiable southerner from the province of Brabant. Brabant and Limburg were the only two provinces in the Netherlands that still celebrated Carnival. Their beer was world famous. Kuster was completely at home in lively Amsterdam. He beckoned to the two inspectors.

"There's a guy who has been waiting for you for almost an hour. I sent him upstairs. I was going to send him away, but Meindert told me you would still be back."

DeKok nodded.

"What sort of man?"

Kuster pulled a face.

"Looks like a bottom feeder. Rich clothes, but no taste. Uses more perfume than a brothel. Not my type."

DeKok laughed.

"Do you have a name?"

"Of course, I do. His name is Haarveld, Willy Haarveld."

DeKok looked at his visitor after he had invited him to sit down next to his desk. Kuster was right. Willy Haarveld was all flash. His clothes were couture, but unmatched. He'd combined canary yellow trousers topped by an aubergine jacket. An embroidered shirt without tie, showed under the jacket. Willy wore a large platinum ring set with diamonds, vulgar and ostentatious. His musky, cloyingly sweet, perfume overtook the room.

DeKok sighed and sank down in his own chair. He observed the other's face with a sharp look. Willy had full, sensuous lips over a weak chin, and a round, fleshy nose. His bleached, lacquered hair framed a face unmistakably made-up. The combination was revolting. DeKok's face and voice were neutral, as he spoke.

"I'm sorry you had to wait," began DeKok, "We weren't expecting you."

Haarveld shook his head in dismissal.

"I had hoped to meet you. The officer downstairs said you were definitely coming back." He stretched out a hand to the inspector. "You, eh, you're Inspector DeKok, aren't you?"

DeKok nodded.

"With kay-oh-kay … at your service."

It sounded mocking.

Willy Haarveld smiled politely.

"I've been told that you are in charge of the case concerning those two boys."

"Which boys?"

"It's about the ones who were strangled yesterday. It's all over the papers. They lived in the same boardinghouse."

DeKok nodded, not committing himself.

"We're handling the case," he merely said.

Haarveld coughed, a timid, discrete little cough, as if to ask for attention.

"Do you know anything about the perpetrator?"

"No."

"Is there a connection between the two murders?"

DeKok grinned.

"There could be. Are you a reporter?"

"No, no," said the visitor hastily. "No, I'm interested, that's all."

DeKok smiled grimly.

"Very well," he said, "I always feel better when I do the questioning. What is your interest?"

Haarveld moved in his chair.

"That is to say …" he played with the embroidered frill on his shirt. "I think I may have met one of the boys, at one time or another."

"Where?"

"In my house, in Laren."

"When?"

Haarveld grinned nervously.

"A few weeks ago, I think. I don't remember the exact date. I am a very busy man, you see. I'm an impresario, a promoter, if you will. I organize stage plays, launch cabaret groups, arrange shows for orchestras and other artists. My clients are under contract and they have to work. If I cannot find them work, they don't eat." He fell silent and took a deep breath. "I also consider it part of my job to make sure each performer has a good repertoire." He raised both hands in the air. "Fresh material is key. So I'm always on the look-out for new texts, songs, melodies, you understand?"

DeKok leaned forward.

"And in that context you've met one of them?"

"Yes."

"Who?"

The impresario made an apologetic gesture.

"That," he said, "I don't know. We might have been

introduced—I certainly did not write his name down. An acquaintance of mine called him 'Mr. Melody.' My friend knew I was always looking for new talent; he sent the boy over to see me."

"And?"

"What do you mean?"

DeKok did not change his demeanor.

"Did you work out an agreement? Did Mr. Melody have material that appealed to you?"

Haarveld hesitated over his answer. He raised both hands in front of his face and brought his fingertips together in a studied gesture.

"He was a strange boy ... man, I should say," he answered softly. "Difficult to understand. He did not know a single note of music, did not play a single instrument, but he said he had melodies in his head. I laughed at him and said that melodies in his head were useless to me. Then he said: 'If you can get them out, you'll make a fortune.'"

"And did you?"

"Did I what?"

"Make a fortune?"

Haarveld was now clearly irritated.

"Have you ever been able to get a fortune out of somebody's head?"

DeKok shook his head calmly.

"No, but I'm not an impresario."

It sounded sarcastic. The old inspector had not yet overcome his distaste for the visitor. Not to mention, the heavy perfume lined his nostrils and reddened his eyes. He fell back in his chair and yawned openly.

"I still do not understand," he said slowly, "why you wanted to see me at this time of the night."

With a sudden motion, Haarveld sat up straight in his chair.

"To disassociate myself."

"What are you talking about?"

"I want nothing to do with the whole mess. I know so well how cops think. You find out the boy visited Laren, you're knocking on my door."

DeKok's eyebrows took on a life of their own. They actually rippled across his forehead. Vledder watched with fascination the effect on Haarveld. But for once, DeKok's eyebrow gymnastics had no effect. Haarveld was too occupied with himself to pay attention to anyone in his surroundings.

For the first time Vledder felt DeKok was actually aware of what happened on his face. Always, the extraordinary behavior of DeKok's eyebrows seemed involuntary. DeKok was generally unaware but, this time, he waited for the effect. Vledder waited. But DeKok calmly posed the next question as if there had been no hesitation at all.

"Sounds like guilt to me. Well, did you do it?" asked DeKok.

Haarveld's face grew scarlet and he began to sweat, streaking his makeup and turning it chalky.

"No," he cried out. He made a high-pitched, nasal protest. "No, I did not do it. I had nothing to do with it. Do you hear me? I had nothing to do with it."

"Then why should you be worried about it?" asked DeKok calmly.

Haarveld let out a deep, theatrical sigh.

"I'm well aware of my own reputation," he said with a studied weariness. "I know people judge me. They gossip. They speculate. It's open season—I'm not exactly irreproachable." It was difficult to tell whether he was bragging or whining. If you look in your records, you'll find I've been accused of theft, corruption, unethical business practices ... even plagiarism."

DeKok grinned broadly.

"Plagiarism of music?"

The impresario nodded slowly.

"Recently, some ape took a shot at me with a rifle. I was lucky. He missed by a few inches, or I wouldn't be here today."

"Do you know who that was?"

"No."

DeKok gave his visitor a searching look.

"Perhaps someone who fancied you had stolen his music?"

"Possibly."

"The police found nothing?"

"I don't think so. I never heard about it again."

DeKok leaned forward again. Some of his distaste for the man had disappeared.

"Again, why did you come here tonight?"

Haarveld did not answer.

DeKok penetrated further into the cloud of perfume. The light green eyes of the promoter came closer.

"Mr. Haarveld, why did you come here tonight?"

The repetition was polite but insistent.

The impresario swallowed hard.

"My fear drove me ... I'm afraid for my life."

With shaking hands he felt around in an inside pocket of the aubergine jacket. He took out an envelope and gave it to DeKok.

"I found this, I found this in my letter box earlier this week."

DeKok took the letter out of the envelope and folded it open. He read out loud: "Keep your filthy hands off Mr. Melody's divine music. The second shot won't miss."

8

When the pimped-out impresario had left, Vledder regarded his colleague with amazement.

"Who could have written that letter?"

DeKok leaned back in his chair and placed his feet on the desk. He was tired. Sleep deprivation took over, making him bone weary. He waved vaguely in Vledder's direction.

"Think about it. What conditions must the letter writer satisfy?"

"I don't understand."

DeKok raised the fingers of his right hand in the air and counted demonstratively.

"One, he must know Mr. Melody exists; which implies he knows Jean-Paul Stappert, or has known him. Two, he has to know Jean-Paul is known for his head full of melodies. Three, the letter writer is familiar with the music and identifies it as 'divine.' Four, he knows Jean-Paul, as 'Mr. Melody,' has been in contact with Haarveld. Five, he knows the impresario by reputation and knows about the recent shooting."

Vledder was full of admiration.

"What a summation," he exclaimed, "how did you manage to explain it all as clearly as you have? You must not be as brain dead as I am at this moment."

DeKok took his legs off the desk and ambled over to the peg to get his raincoat and his hat. He placed the hat on his head and bundled the raincoat under an arm. Near the door he turned around.

"See you in the morning."

It almost sounded like a threat.

A glorious new day broke. The friendly summer sun caressed the Damrak and made Central Station look like a fairy palace. The flags on the docks waved gaily in the slight breeze, announcing tour boats and water taxis. They added a festive look for crowds waiting to see Amsterdam from the water.

DeKok enjoyed himself. Despite his city's many dark sides, he loved Amsterdam. It was a deep and abiding love that had strengthened over years. Amsterdam remained, for him, a place where everything was possible and anything could start. A Calvinist to his core he found it never reconciled Amsterdam's extremes with her beauty. Change kept him young, and serving in criminal investigation kept his mental processes from the atrophy of age.

Whistling cheerfully he entered the station house.

Much to his surprise he found Vledder already at his desk. The young inspector sat listlessly in his chair, his expression, annoyed. DeKok approached.

"What's the matter? Sleep badly?"

Vledder shook his head.

"The commissaris has been here several times already and was asking for you. He wanted to know where you were."

"And?"

"I told him we were here rather late last night, as well as the previous night, so you were a little later than usual."

DeKok looked at the clock.

"It's barely ten o'clock," he said, surprised. "What does the man want?"

"He wants to talk to you. He was agitated—wanted to know if we had filed any reports regarding the two murders."

DeKok shook his head.

"Other than the original contact report stating we've found the bodies, we've made no reports. You know that. We haven't had the time."

Vledder looked embarrassed.

"That's what I told him. He ripped into me, started to curse me and called us bunglers."

"What?"

Vledder nodded.

"That's what he said."

Something seemed to snap inside DeKok. He turned on his heel and stomped out of the room. Vledder came from behind his desk and ran after him. He was too late. As he reached the corridor, DeKok had already entered the room of the commissaris.

Startled, Commissaris Buitendam looked up from the papers on his desk when DeKok suddenly appeared at the other side of the desk. The expression on DeKok's face portended no good. Buitendam knew well the signs of barely contained anger.

The commissaris coughed importantly and tried to project dignity and authority.

"I don't think I heard you knock."

DeKok grinned broadly. The berserk rage that had momentarily seized him slipped into the background.

"I take serious exception to the word 'bungling,' as it relates to our efforts." It still sounded sharp and emotional. "I demand an explanation."

Commissaris Buitendam nodded. There was a sorrowful look on his face.

"That was unjust and insulting," he said softly. "My temper got the upper hand—it was out of control." He looked up at DeKok and sighed, "The thing is, DeKok, could you not keep me apprised of developments? In my position this results in some painfully embarrassing exchanges."

"Two young men have been murdered," answered DeKok evenly. "One was strangled in a boardinghouse on Prince Henry Quay, the second near Emperor's Canal. The facts have been reported and an APB with all the known facts of the original contact has been forwarded. Everything known about the cases was reported. There is no more to be said at this time."

The commissaris took a deep breath.

"But that was two days ago. I want further details."

DeKok's answer was curt.

"There are no further details."

Buitendam's pale face regained some color.

"Mr. Schaap, the judge-advocate in this case, demands details. He's the instructing magistrate in this matter. The father of one of the victims, a Mr. Bavel, has approached him. Bavel wants information and demands that the case be solved forthwith."

Despairing, DeKok gripped his head with both hands.

"Mr. Bavel," he said with a grimace. "While he was alive,

Mr. Bavel never even bothered about his son Erik ... practically abandoned him. So what does he want *after* his death?"

The commissaris waved an elegant, slender hand in dismissal.

"Those are matters that do not concern us," he said casually. "If Mr. Bavel demands to know the circumstances surrounding his son's death, then we must respond to his request."

DeKok obstinately shook his head.

"The rich and, no doubt, influential Mr. Bavel will hear no details from me, not a moment before I have determined a motive and identified his son's killer."

Buitendam's anger returned. There was a determined look in his eyes.

"You don't decide that," he almost screamed. "If Mr. Schaap wants to furnish information, he will. He is the judicial leader of this investigation. He is entitled."

DeKok grinned mischievously.

"Leader of the investigation," he blurted. "Maybe we could send the great jurist back to the Boy Scouts." He rubbed his nose thoughtfully. "Perhaps they can train him to be assistant patrol leader."

The commissaris suddenly came out of his chair. His eyes flashed and his nostrils quivered. With an enraged gesture he pointed at the door.

"OUT!"

DeKok left.

Vledder gave his mentor a searching look.

"Is he still alive?"

"Who?"

Vledder thumbed over his shoulder.

"The commissaris, of course. When you stomped out of the room, I thought you were going to kill him. Really, I even tried to stop you."

DeKok laughed.

"No, I bungled it," He couldn't resist.

Vledder smiled.

"I know you too well to be telling you about his antics. I should never have told you." He shook his head. "But what did he want, actually?"

"Apparently rich Pa Bavel has friends in high places. Through the judge-advocate he seeks particulars about the death of his son and demands the case be solved at once."

"Our boss got nervous?"

"First *his* boss got nervous."

"And?"

"What?"

"Did he get the details?"

DeKok shook his head with determination.

"You know," said Vledder, "I can whip up a series of reports from the last few days in no time at all."

DeKok nodded. He knew that all pertinent information was kept in Vledder's computer. He also knew that Vledder had programmed his computer to spit out a report on almost any subject by merely merging standard language with new factoids. He'd programmed the system to make even a coffee break seem an important event. Vledder knew all the tricks and requirements of the large police bureaucracy. He knew how to play the game. But DeKok would have nothing of it. He kept relying on tried and proven methods developed before the computer age. When DeKok delivered his final report, it was stripped of all extraneous matter and almost always resulted in a conviction.

"I won't even consider it," he said after short pause. "They have what they have and that's all they get until I have more concrete information."

Vledder raised a finger.

"You are such a diplomat."

DeKok ignored the remark.

"I told Buitendam that I had no further details ... told him all I knew was contained in the original report and the APB."

"And he swallowed that?"

DeKok grinned.

"He had no choice. Besides, I really have no idea in which direction to look for the killer."

"Ramon Bavel?"

For a moment DeKok looked puzzled.

"Who?"

Vledder nodded with emphasis.

"Ramon Bavel ... he's taking music lessons."

With a derisive snort DeKok sat down in his chair.

"It's part of a liberal education. Somehow I'm not surprised to learn that Ramon is taking music lessons."

Vledder smiled secretly.

"Perhaps I can supply the surprise. Do you know who his teacher is?"

"Well?"

"Alex Waardenburg."

DeKok leaned forward.

"Now that *is* a surprise. How did you find that out?"

Vledder smiled smugly.

"I've been interested in Ramon Bavel since his mother told us about him."

DeKok reflected.

"Oh, yes, he's the heir now, to the Bavel fortune."

Vledder nodded.

"Exactly. As far as I'm concerned, Ramon is a potential killer. I called the local police in Heemstede this morning. I have a colleague there who went to the academy with me. I asked him what they knew about the Bavel family."

"And?"

Vledder punched up a screen on his computer.

"There's quite bit," he said, one eye on the computer and the other on his written notes. Apparently Erik and Ricky caused a lot of trouble for the local police while they were addicted. They committed thefts, breaking and entering, even an aggravated robbery. It was always Ma Bavel who defended her sons. Pa Bavel treated the two more like stepsons. He started turning his back while they were little."

"And Ramon?"

Vledder shook his head.

"Ramon has no police record. If he did anything wrong, he was under the radar."

DeKok reflected in silence.

"But how," he asked after a long pause, "did your colleague know Ramon is taking music lessons in Amsterdam?"

Vledder laughed. There was a sense of triumph in his voice.

"My friend and Ramon are members of the same tennis club."

"Tennis?"

Vledder nodded with a broad grin.

"Tennis, that's right."

9

Vledder was getting enthusiastic.

"Shall we pick him up?"

"Who?"

"Ramon Bavel. If we play it just right with Heemstede, we can pick him up—no problem."

DeKok slowly shook his head.

"I'd leave it, for the time being. He'd walk in a few hours, regardless. That is, if we could even get an arrest warrant with what we have."

Vledder looked exasperated.

"He plays tennis," he exclaimed. "Dr. Koning said it … strong hands … someone who has developed a strong grip."

Again DeKok shook his head.

"It's not enough. Knowing our esteemed judge-advocate, he wouldn't even entertain it. If it came up later, he'd develop amnesia."

Vledder stood up and came over to DeKok's desk.

"Ramon has a motive," he groaned. "Based on the size of the Bavel estate, times three, it's a helluva motive. The whole addiction test scenario indicates he wanted Erik and Ricky incapacitated or dead. Now he's not just top dog, he's the lone heir."

DeKok sighed.

"You're right, Dick," he said wearily. "Everything points to Ramon. But we have no proof. Without judicial proof, something that will stand up in court, we don't stand a chance. Think for a moment about his father's influence."

Vledder sat down on the corner of DeKok's desk.

"But that's it exactly," he pleaded. "Pa Bavel never showed any interest in his younger sons, even when they were too young to get into serious scrapes. Now, suddenly, he turns the heat on the big wigs. Small wonder our commissaris gets nervous. To what end?" He grinned crookedly, "Old man Bavel sees a cloud hanging over his favorite, Ramon." The young inspector leaned closer over the desk. "It's as clear as crystal. Even the mother stops just short of saying she knows Ramon had something to do with the murder of his brother Erik."

DeKok smiled.

"You sound very convincing," he admitted. "And there are some elements of truth in what you say, but—"

Vledder interrupted sharply.

"No, it's all true. Believe me. If we don't take steps immediately, Ramon will have vanished. Or he'll have an army of lawyers who will help him to build a wall of lies." He sputtered, swept up in his own emotions. "That … that … we can't allow that to happen. No, we have to do *something*."

DeKok rubbed his neck. Some of the fire in Vledder's argument lit a spark in his own thinking. If he did what he felt deep down, he'd be on the way to Heemstede at this very moment to arrest Ramon. But an inner voice told him to wait. He did not have the entire picture. A vital piece of the puzzle was missing. Loose ends disquieted him. He could not reconcile the crime, the perpetrator, and the motive with the facts—these elements lacked unity. Until he could grasp the connection between cause and effect, an arrest would be precipitous. In this job the facts had to come first. They absolutely had to proceed in an orderly manner.

He looked up at Vledder. Vledder's face was tense and intent. DeKok closed his eyes for a moment.

"Justice, my boy," he said in a gentle, almost fatherly tone of voice, "is an illusion. You'll never find it, no matter how long you look. We don't serve justice with a capital 'J' but with set rules and regulations that we call 'the law.' That's the distinction. For now we have to keep hands off Ramon." He smiled wanly. "Meanwhile Bavel and his son may soon commit a blunder that will give us a better grip. But as it stands—"

DeKok did not finish the sentence. From the corner of his eye he noticed a tall young man being ushered to his desk by one of the other detectives. The young visitor was in his mid-twenties and athletic looking. He wore a dark-blue blazer and grey flannel trousers. The neon light made his blond hair shine.

"Would you speak with me," he said softly. "About Jean-Paul … Jean-Paul Stappert."

DeKok nodded encouragingly and invited the young man to seat himself. Vledder discreetly moved to his own desk.

The young man sat down, placing his long, slender hands on his knees.

"I had to work up the courage to come here," he said.

"Why is that?"

He looked contrite.

"Warmoes Street has a very tough reputation."

DeKok waved that away.

"That reputation is not justified. We're the most friendly, accommodating officers you can imagine. We're all 'Uncle' Police here." The he caught himself. "I'm sorry, I haven't introduced myself." It sounded sincere. "My name is DeKok ... DeKok with kay-oh-kay." He hesitated a moment and then added: "And with whom do I have the pleasure?"

The young man extended a hand.

"Kiliaan ... Kiliaan Waardenburg."

"Are you related to Alex Waardenburg?"

The young man nodded.

"My father."

DeKok and Vledder gave the young man a second look.

"Your father," said DeKok, "was here yesterday."

"I know that, yes. He told me about his visit."

"And does he know you're here?"

Kiliaan seemed to hesitate.

"That's hard to say," he said after along pause. "He may or may not know."

"Did you tell him?"

"No."

DeKok looked surprised.

"Then, how can he know?"

Kiliaan Waardenburg moved uneasily in his chair.

"Sometimes ... it's like my father is a telepath. It's a bit of a bore, really. When he reads my thoughts it's as if I cease to exist as an entity ... as if I'm just an extension of him. My mother doesn't share my concern. We've talked about it. She retains her identity within her relationship with my father. Not me, not quite. All I can do is think clearly and concisely when I'm around him."

DeKok cocked his head to one side.

"What does that mean ... clearly and concisely."

Young Waardenburg stared into the distance.

"It means to eliminate every bad and sinful thought."

"Is that possible?"

Kiliaan nodded with emphasis.

"Yes, you can train yourself. First you eliminate all thought. You ban all ideas and empty your mind, then, slowly you fill it up again. While you do that you think only pure thoughts—God, for instance or music."

Although the explanation did not satisfy DeKok in the least, he decided to leave the subject of "clear thinking" aside for the moment.

"Are you following in your father's footsteps?"

"How do you mean?"

"Are you going to be a musician, as well?"

"I play the piano."

"Professionally?"

"Indeed. I'm with the Municipal Symphonic Orchestra."

"Your father's orchestra?"

Waardenburg sighed.

"He introduced me. I'm very grateful for that. It's been a good experience. But I prefer to perform solo. My father and others who would know, say I have talent; they predict a great future for me as a pianist." He grinned shyly. "Myself, I'm not so sure. I'm more and more drawn to composition."

"And what does your father think about that?"

Kiliaan almost shrugged.

"Father is not too happy about it. He insists I continue my piano studies." He paused and looked pensively at his hands. "I don't understand his aversion," he continued.

"When he was younger, he wrote several compositions himself."

"Were they successful?"

Kiliaan Waardenburg pursed his lips and shook his head slowly.

"Not really," he said slowly. "They were not melodic. Father is very staid and dogmatic—also in his music."

DeKok listened carefully to Kiliaan's tone.

"Is that why he has remained as second fiddle?"

Kiliaan looked up. For the first time there was a hard look on his face.

"You are way off base," he said sharply. "Playing the second violin is not unimportant. On the contrary, only in casual conversation has 'second fiddle' become something trivial."

It sounded reproving.

DeKok showed his most endearing smile. There was something likeable about the young man.

"We digress. You came to talk about the death of Jean-Paul Stappert."

"Indeed."

"Did you know him?"

"Yes."

"Casually? I mean as just another of your father's students?"

Young Waardenburg shook his head.

"Jean-Paul and I were friends, more or less. We were always discussing music. Jean-Paul was very talented. Music to him was not something that came from outside ... not something you learn, but a complete inner life. You see music was part of his being from birth."

DeKok rubbed his face with both hands. He was conscious of the enthusiasm in the young man's voice.

"You admired Jean-Paul?"

"Yes, a lot."

"Why?'

Kiliaan Waardenburg made a vague gesture.

"As I said, he had a unique gift for creating melodies almost effortlessly." He shook his head sadly. "There are not many truly creative spirits."

DeKok nodded to himself.

"Did Jean-Paul tell you he was going to contact Willy Haarveld?"

"Yes," said Kiliaan somberly, lowering his head. "He was actually eager. I told him that Willy was a low-life. My father knows him as well. He's a swindler."

"And did Jean-Paul listen to you?"

"No," smiled Kiliaan. "No, Jean-Paul was impervious. 'Nobody swindles me,' he said, 'not any more.'"

DeKok stared at the ceiling for a while. Thoughtfully he rubbed the bridge of his nose with a little finger.

"Did you ever visit Jean-Paul in his boardinghouse?"

His visitor nodded.

"I've been there two, maybe three times."

"Did you meet Erik?"

Kiliaan smiled sorrowfully.

"I had limited contact with him. He was sort of reticent, vague. I never understood how Jean-Paul became friends with him. They had so little in common. Erik did not care for music at all."

Vledder, who had kept in the background, taking careful notes and listening intently, suddenly interrupted.

"So Erik was completely different from Ramon?"

Kiliaan Gave Vledder a surprised look.

"Ramon? What's the matter with Ramon?"

"You know Ramon?" asked Vledder.

Kiliaan raised his hands.

"He's one of my father's students, has been for years. He plays the clarinet."

"That's all you know about him?"

"Yes. We've met. He left me cold—he's several years older, so we didn't really connect. Anyway, I have very little contact with most of my father's students. Jean-Paul was an exception."

Vledder was relentless.

"What *do* you know about Ramon?"

Waardenburg grimaced.

"He pays big tuition. According to father he's from a very rich family."

"Do you know the family name?"

"No."

"Bavel."

Kiliaan Waardenburg sighed, oblivious.

"Bavel," he repeated tonelessly. "Yes, I think that was the name."

"He was Erik's brother," said Vledder, almost accusing.

Kiliaan was confused. He looked at Vledder uncertainly.

"That ... eh, I didn't know that," he laughed sheepishly. "It's hard to believe. They don't look at all alike."

Vledder ignored that.

"How often did Bavel come for lessons?"

"Erik had lessons a few times a week."

"Did he have an appointment on the same day that Jean-Paul was killed?"

Young Waardenburg did not answer at once. He looked thoughtfully at the ceiling. But after a few seconds he nodded.

"Yes, yes, I remember. Ramon also had a study session that day, earlier in the evening."

Vledder leaned forward.

"So, it's possible that Ramon did not go home afterward, but waited near Emperor's Canal for Jean-Paul to appear."

The young man laughed nervously.

"I can't imagine why he would? Jean-Paul did not even know Ramon, as far as I know. I don't think that they knew each other."

Vledder held the visitor's eyes with his own.

"But it is possible?"

Kiliaan Waardenburg sighed again. The questions seemed to irritate him.

"Sure," he admitted reluctantly. "Everything's possible."

Vledder leaned even closer.

"So, Ramon Bavel could have enticed your friend to the side of the canal and, then, he could have strangled him between the parked cars."

Kiliaan looked at Vledder with wide-open eyes. He was suddenly very pale.

"What ... what are you after? What, what do you want?" he stuttered.

Vledder's answer was terse.

"I'm who's left after a murder and I want the killer," he said.

10

DeKok indicated to Kiliaan he could leave. The young man was visibly shaken. DeKok accompanied him to the door. After that he returned to his desk and shook his head at Vledder.

"That was a bad interrogation," he said with disapproval in his voice. "I thought I had taught you better than that."

Vledder snorted, not at all contrite. The tension was still evident in his face. His eyes were wild and the large artery in his neck was swollen and visibly throbbing with anger.

"I'm after the truth," he said defensively.

DeKok pointed a finger at his young colleague.

"No, my boy. Truth is a tricky matter. You're only looking for the truth according to Vledder. An inspector of police recognizes the distinction. You've convinced yourself Ramon is the perp. Along the way you've compromised your objectivity. You never gave Kiliaan any space, or even allowed him to think. He couldn't express his own opinions or feelings. So you succeeded in robbing him of the opportunity to formulate his own arguments. That's wrong. For a professional it's almost unforgivable."

Vledder sighed deeply.

"Ramon is the killer," he said decisively. "Believe me. It went just as I said. He was waiting for Jean-Paul and strangled him. Only after that, did he go to the boarding-house to take care of Erik."

DeKok shook his head sadly.

"May I reiterate? It was a bad interrogation. This time I restrained myself, because I feel a young person must be allowed to make a mistake, once in a while."

"Mistake?"

DeKok nodded as he sank into his chair.

"What is the net worth of your interrogation? The only concrete fact you got is Ramon had a music lesson on the night of the murders. That's it! Once you got to that point you should have stopped. It was all downhill from there—everything you forced on Kiliaan afterward was damaging to our investigation."

Vledder snorted again.

"I didn't force anything on him. I merely described how it had happened."

DeKok waved that away.

"How you *think* it happened," he corrected. "As of now we have nothing—no evidence to make your theory reality." He paused, "I hope Alex Waardenburg knows how to keep his mouth shut."

"Whatever do you mean?"

DeKok ran his fingers through his hair.

"If Kiliaan discusses our conversation with his father (or his father uses his "psychic powers") and the senior Waardenburg then discusses it with Pa Bavel we have a problem. Worse, if anyone discusses it with the press, we've had it." He fell silent. "I can just see the headlines now," he continued after a while. "Warmoes Street police identify Ramon Bavel as killer. Well, in that case the fecal matter will surely connect with the rotary blades. Everybody will be after your hide, including Schaap. Then you can retire before you take any action against Ramon."

Vledder chewed his lower lip. The expression on his face was contrite.

"You're right," he said, "That's obvious. I never thought about that."

DeKok got up and placed a consoling hand on Vledder's shoulder. He felt Vledder's anguish. As a young officer he had too often been quick to judge, rushing for an abstract finish line. He carried some bruises on his soul because of it.

"Don't let it get you down too much," he consoled. "I speak from experience in this regard." Then he grinned brightly. "After all, experience is the name we give to the sum of our mistakes." The grin changed into a cheerful chuckle. "Come on, we're off to Utrecht."

He turned away and gathered his hat and raincoat from the peg on the wall.

Vledder hastened after him.

"Utrecht?" he asked in stunned amazement.

DeKok nodded.

"Yes, Utrecht, It's the domicile of Long Jack, aka Skinny Jack, aka Hague Jack … or just Jaap Santen."

As they left the city in their old VW, heavy raindrops made rivulets down the windshield. Vledder activated the wipers and fog lights.

"What do you want with Jaap Santen, or Long Jack, or whatever his name is?" asked Vledder.

DeKok smiled.

"I want to talk to him."

"What about?"

"Destruction."

"What is this?" asked Vledder. "Twenty questions?"

"No, but it's against the law. Article 350 of the General Code," lectured DeKok, "to willfully and illegally destroy pillows and mattresses."

"There's no such law," Vledder had to laugh.

"No, but there should be. The law actually covers all vandalism, so why not pillows and mattresses?"

Vledder almost rear-ended another car that suddenly stopped at the intersection with Rose's Canal.

"All right, whatever," Vledder's tone was sardonic. "But is he, indeed guilty? Long Jack, I mean?"

"Absolutely—he and his partner, Jan Rouwen both did this. But we don't have a regular address for Rouwen. He sometimes stays with his old mother in St. Jozef Lane. He frequents the High Catherine Shopping Mall. But Jaap Santen lives in Utrecht, 397 Jan Dijk Street, on the second floor. He is the tall, skinny guy Mina Lyons identified. She swore she would recognize him."

Vledder was surprised.

"How did you figure that out?"

DeKok did not answer. He slid down in the seat until his eyes were just level with the top of the dashboard. The rhythmic sweeps of the wipers lulled him. He yawned and pulled his hat down over his eyes.

"I forgot to tell you," he said finally. "Frans Kruger called me the morning after the murders to say he had been unable to find a single fingerprint in the room occupied by Bavel, not even his or Jean-Paul's prints."

"But they should have been there."

"Yes, unless somebody carefully wiped down everything in the room."

"Someone wanted to eliminate their own prints."

"Clearly."

"The killer?"

DeKok yawned again.

"Not necessarily. It could have been done by someone who entered the room after Erik's murder."

"But what would be the purpose?"

DeKok pursed his lips.

"Perhaps it was preventive—someone was uncomfortable having us get a good set of what he, or she, thought were the killer's prints."

Vledder fell silent, thinking it over. DeKok's observations intrigued him. Although he had now worked with the gray sleuth for years, he still found it hard to come to grips with some of his partners confounding statements.

They drove on in silence for a long while.

Then DeKok suddenly asked: "Did I ever tell you about Kleutermans?

"No, who's he?"

"He was my mentor when I first started as a young constable."

Vledder was intrigued. DeKok seldom talked about his early days, other than in the vaguest of terms.

"What about him?"

"I happened to meet him last week," said DeKok. "He's long since retired, but in those days he was a giant of man ... a man with a natural dominance and respected by every one. He did his duty, walked his beat with an unquenchable joviality. But there was one thing he hated with a passion. He hated writing reports and he hated to give out tickets."

"Aha," said Vledder, "I see, *that* is where you learned that."

"Maybe. But he especially disliked tickets. His motto

used to be: 'A ticket is a defeat.' He felt that a good policeman never should have to write a ticket. And if, for whatever reason, you *have* to write a ticket, it's an admission of failure."

"Wow, a strange attitude for a uniformed constable."

"Well, that is as may be. But I can assure you that Kleutermans suffered few defeats in his long career."

"I take it, this is leading somewhere?"

"I was reminded of the time we got a new boss. A brand, spanking new inspector, young and full of ambition. He summoned Kleutermans and told him that he had gone over the records and was amazed to find how few tickets Kleutermans had written. 'That will have to change,' he said. 'You must be stricter. I like solid tickets.'"

"He was big on fines?"

"Yes. Anyway, Kleutermans left without saying anything. About a week later he wrote one of his rare tickets. He made out the ticket very carefully. In those days we did not have pre-printed forms, you see. The officer had to write it all out in longhand, almost like a letter. It actually was a mini-report. When he had it all finished, he carefully glued the report to a large paving stone and submitted it to the new boss."

"'What's the meaning of this?' the inspector asked. Kleutermans shrugged his shoulders. 'You said you liked a solid ticket and that's the largest stone I could find.'"

Vledder laughed so hard, he almost lost control of the car.

"Kleutermans also refused," continued DeKok, "to issue parking tickets. For that we had pre-printed forms. It was therefore a simple, quick thing to do. But Kleutermans decided that the issuing of parking tickets was unworthy of a real policeman. There was no personal contact, you see."

"So he was the reason we now have meter maids?"

"Could be. But one day the same young inspector ordered Kleutermans to ticket a street full of illegally parked cars. He came back, more than an hour later, without having written a single parking ticket. The inspector was as mad as our own commissaris sometimes gets."

"Only in your case," interjected Vledder.

"Am I telling this story, or are you?"

"Sorry, go on."

"Well, as I said, the inspector was very angry. Kleutermans shrugged his shoulders. 'I tried,' he said, 'but I couldn't get farther than the first car. There was no way I could put a ticket under the wiper. I tried and tried, but the driver had forgotten to shut off the windshield wipers.'"

Vledder laughed again. They had already crossed the new bridge across the Amstel on the way to Utrecht.

"It came to mind right away," said DeKok, "when I met him last week. He was thinner and a little more stooped, but the fiery look in his eyes was the same. 'Much trouble with corruption, these days?' he asked. I reacted vaguely. 'You know,' he said, 'that reminds me of the time someone tried to bribe me. It was a bar fight. I finally managed to get the drunk outside. He was the belligerent type, who had pestered other patrons. Once we were in the street he gave me *rijksdaalder*, two and a half guilders. That was a lot of money in those days, real silver. You could buy a lot with one of those. I took the coin, bent down, and rolled it down the street.' He grinned like a little boy at the thought. 'That guy went chasing after it. I've never seen a drunk run that hard or fast. Finally he fell right on top of the coin.' 'So, no defeat,' I said. He laughed. 'Not for me—I didn't do the belly flop.'"

DeKok fell silent. They were approaching Utrecht, the city of the same name in the center of the province of Utrecht, the province in the center of Holland. Vledder glanced aside. Suddenly he had a baffled look on his face.

"Now I still don't know," he exclaimed, "how you decided on Jaap Santen."

DeKok pushed his hat farther back on his head.

"After those two guys visited the rooming house, I asked Kruger to check the rooms out again."

"Aha," exclaimed Vledder. "And that's when he found the new prints."

"As simple as that," smiled DeKok.

Jan Dijk Street in Utrecht turned out to be a street that ran parallel to a rail dike. Every once in a while a train would come flying past with a deafening noise.

Vledder parked the Beetle a few houses past number 379 and got out. DeKok followed him laboriously. The space in the passenger seat was really not large enough for his tall, 200-pound frame. With longing he recalled the time of the canal boats. In those days he could have made the trip comfortably ensconced in a snug cabin. He would have arrived fresh and vitalized by a long nap. When he finally unfolded himself from the car and stretched a little, Vledder locked the doors.

The weather broke. It stopped raining and, every once in a while, the sun peeked through the clouds. It gave the somber palette of the street a little color.

The front door of 379 was ajar. DeKok pushed it open and climbed the wooden stairs to the second floor. The railing was greasy and the treads creaked under his weight.

Vledder followed.

It was pitch dark in the second floor corridor. A faint streak of light crept from under a door on the landing. DeKok paused to accustom his eyes to the darkness. Slowly the surroundings showed some contours.

The top panel and bottom panels of the apartment entrance carried fresh scars. The cracks and dents were left by someone trying to enter forcibly.

DeKok smiled grimly. Carefully he tried the doorknob and pushed. The door did not budge.

With a shrug, DeKok put a hand in a pocket and produced a small brass cylinder. He made some adjustments to the cylinder and gave silent thanks to Handy Henkie, an ex-burglar who had gifted him with the useful tool.

In a gesture of horror, Vledder covered his eyes with both hands.

DeKok looked at him in surprise.

"What's the matter with you?" he whispered.

"Vledder shook his head.

"I don't want to be a witness."

"Now what?"

"I don't want to be a witness to breaking and entering."

DeKok smiled. Vledder's scruples sometimes amused him. DeKok felt no pangs of conscience as he sorted out the right combination. He leaned towards Vledder.

"With just the law in your hand, you don't open many doors," he said softly. He raised the little instrument in the air. "But with this I am Ali Baba."

He applied the instrument to the lock in the door.

"Open Sesame," he whispered after a few seconds. With a nonchalant gesture he replaced the instrument in his pocket and pushed against the now unlocked door.

He took a step back and with a polite bow invited Vledder to enter.

The front door let right into the kitchen. From there they reached a sparsely furnished living room. An old sofa and an easy chair were grouped behind a round coffee table. The material on the sofa and chairs was worn. An ashtray on the table was filled with cigarette butts. Some had brown plastic mouthpieces with red lipstick.

On a dresser without doors they saw a large color television set. Next to the TV were the telephone and a telephone directory. It was one of those old-fashioned metal contraptions that would open at the required letter by moving an arrow up or down the side.

The bedroom was a mess. There was no bed. Large tufts of kapok leaked out of the mattress that was placed on the floor. There were no sheets, no pillowcases, just a few dirty blankets. Pieces of clothing were spread along the floor.

Vledder sighed.

"Nobody home," he said. He followed DeKok back to the living room. "Do you want to wait here for Santen?" he asked.

DeKok shook his head.

"No, I don't think so. We better lock up and leave everything as we found it. We can wait for him in the car. Santen is remarkably tall and thin—has a gaunt look. He's easy to spot."

"Do you have a description of Jan Rouwen, his partner?"

DeKok nodded.

"Rouwen is a little blond guy with an average face. To give himself *some* personality he is trying to grow some hair on his upper lip."

Vledder laughed.

"So, he has a moustache?"

"That's a stretch. It may some day be a moustache, but I doubt it."

"You want to first take a look at High Catherine. Perhaps we can find him there and pick him up. If not, we can always get back here."

DeKok did not answer. He pulled his lower lip out and let it plop back. Vledder thought it disgusting, his least endearing mannerism. He had hoped to surprise Santen in his house. A trek through a large shopping mall seemed unappealing.

He turned abruptly and walked back to the room with the telephone. He picked up the phone index, moved the pointer to "H" and pushed the button at the bottom. The top of the device popped open. With a satisfied smile he turned to show the page to Vledder. At the bottom a name was written in with a pencil.

"Haarveld," read Vledder, "Willy Haarveld."

11

Detective-Inspector DeKok of the Amsterdam Municipal Police did not like stake-outs. It was part of the profession, but he could seldom muster the required patience. It was a slow death by boredom. The mere thought of sitting for hours near a certain house, store, or meeting place made him shiver with revulsion. He was known to shamelessly use his seniority only to delegate this chore.

He looked at his watch. It was almost three thirty in the afternoon. They'd been crammed into the VW for more than an hour and a half. Although there were two of them, both kept looking at the house almost the whole time, to no avail.

With a sigh he turned toward Vledder, who seemed calmer than usual.

"I'm getting a concrete backside with all this sitting. Who knows how late Santen will be back. It could be very late."

Vledder shrugged.

"What sort of business do you suppose he has with Willy Haarveld?" He paused. "02153 is the area code for Laren, right?"

DeKok nodded absent-mindedly. He really had no inkling. Direct dialing was another of his prejudices. He preferred to chat with a local operator, then a long-distance operator, eventually reaching his party—so much more civilized.

Vledder was well aware of DeKok's prejudices.

"Good thing I looked it up in the phone book I found in the dresser," he remarked slyly.

DeKok ignored the remark. He moved uneasily in the seat. Vledder slapped the steering wheel.

"This is all too much coincidence," exclaimed Vledder suddenly.

"What?"

Vledder took his eyes off the building they were watching and turned in his seat.

"Let's review the facts, as we know them," began Vledder. "Jean-Paul gets to know Willy Haarveld through Little Lowee. Let's keep aside for the moment that Haarveld, to say the least, is ethically challenged. Jean-Paul offers Haarveld music ... melodies that could net him a small fortune. It takes no time at all for Jean-Paul to end up strangled to death. Right after the murder, Long Jack and his partner trash Jean-Paul's room and the room that belonged to Erik Bavel."

"They did more than trash it, they vandalized it."

"Vandalized it," agreed Vledder impatiently. He raised a finger in the air. "By the time rigor mortis sets in, Willy Haarveld wanders into Warmoes Street in order to protest his innocence." Vledder grinned evilly. "When we search Long Jack's phone contacts, what do we find? I tell you what we *find*—we find Mr. Willy Haarveld's phone number."

DeKok smiled tolerantly.

"So what?"

For a moment Vledder seemed stunned.

"So what? So what?" he asked. "So there is a connection between Jaap Santen, Long Jack, or whoever, and Willy Haarveld." He hesitated for a moment, then, plunged ahead: "And it may mean that Willy Haarveld ordered the vandalizing of the rooms. That's so what," he concluded triumphantly.

DeKok nodded thoughtfully.

"Very good, Dick. But it begs the question: What did Haarveld expect to find in the rooms, or, to be precise, what did he expect the vandals to find?"

Vledder's mouth fell open as he stared at his older partner.

"For one thing, a fortune in melodies," he said finally.

There was a sad expression on DeKok's face as he shook his head.

"No, that does not follow at all. Erik Bavel's room was trashed for no particular reason—he didn't have compositions to steal. Also we know the treasure trove of music was locked up in Jean-Paul's head … a *living* Jean-Paul. What use would he be dead? Jean-Paul was of no—" Suddenly he stopped and pointed out the window.

"Jan … Jan Rouwen."

Vledder stood in the middle of the room. His legs were spread and he rocked slightly back and forth on the balls of his feet. It was the way DeKok often stood in front of the window in the station house. Vledder had appropriated the mannerism from his mentor. He looked down at the young man on the sofa. DeKok was right, he thought. Aside from his short stature, Jan Rouwen was your average guy. He leaned over the suspect.

"Where is Jaap Santen?"

Rouwen shrugged his shoulders.

"He was going away for a few days, he said. Headed across the border. He gave me the key to his apartment. I don't have a place of my own and I don't always want to stay at my mother's. The woman never shuts up ... nags me about work and things."

Vledder nodded.

"When is Jack coming back?"

Jan Rouwen raised his hands in an apologetic gesture.

"I don't know. Really. Jaap plays it close to the vest. He never tells you much. I'll know it when he gets back."

"Do you know Willy Haarveld?"

Rouwen looked dumb.

"Never heard of him," He looked at Vledder. "Should I know him?"

"How did you know it was a man? Willy is usually a girl's name, short for Wilhelmina."

"Come on—it's short for William—funny you don't know any Williams."

Vledder kept his temper admirably, much to DeKok's surprise.

"You're positive. You don't know this particular Willy?"

"Yes, I'm sure. Why wouldn't you believe me?"

"I can't imagine."

Rouwen grimaced.

"You have a picture?"

"What for?"

"A picture of the Wilhelmina or William I'm supposed to know."

DeKok intervened.

"What did Jaap pay you for the job in Amsterdam?"

"What job?"

"The search of those two rooms in a boardinghouse at Prince Henry Quay."

"Never been there."

DeKok grinned.

"Is that so? Why did you think the two of us came all the way to Utrecht, just like that? You think this is a game?" He shook his head. "Here's how it is. We came here because we found fingerprints at a crime scene. Beautiful, clear fingerprints, belonging to you and your pal. They were all over the place. Oh, and the owner can identify both of you."

Jan Rouwen lowered his head.

"Fifty bucks," he said.

DeKok sat down next to him on the sofa.

"That's all?"

"It was a nothing job."

DeKok snorted.

"Long Jack will have gotten a lot more."

Rouwen shrugged again.

"I don't care. That's his business—he pays me to run some errands and I keep my mouth shut."

DeKok shook his head.

"You've been bought and sold my boy," he said in a friendly tone of voice. "Fifty bucks to search the room of a murder victim. Don't you think Jaap is having a nice long vacation in Spain somewhere from his share of whatever you found? How far can you get with your fifty?"

The young man was getting restless.

"It was a nothing job," he repeated loudly. "I told you. Jaap could have done it alone if he'd wanted. He just asked me to come along to Amsterdam for the company. The pay was just a bonus," he glanced at DeKok. "Pretty low risk for me—I just stood around while Jaap searched."

"What was he looking for?"

Rouwen lowered his head again and remained silent.

"What was Long Jack after?"

Rouwen swallowed.

"How would I know? We didn't talk about it."

There was a stubborn look on DeKok's face as he repeated the question.

"What was he looking for?"

Jan Rouwen shook his head vehemently.

"I don't know," he screamed. "I don't know."

With his head still lowered he suddenly jumped up and forward, hitting Vledder hard in the stomach. It was a perfect football tackle. Vledder went backward, smack onto the glass plate of the coffee table. The thick glass gave way with the sound of a pistol shot.

Before DeKok could react, Jan Rouwen ran into the kitchen.

DeKok bolted at full speed, but by the time he had reached the kitchen, the door to the street slammed shut. He turned and ran back into the room.

Vledder picked himself up from among two large pieces of glass. He was unsteady and the color had drained from his face.

Both inspectors stared straight ahead. Their mission to Utrecht had not been very successful. Neither was inclined to talk. The sun and the cheerful cumulus clouds had disappeared. It was raining again. The weather reflected the mood.

DeKok forced himself into a more upright position in the seat. He struggled to keep from nodding off. He looked at Vledder with concern.

"How is it going?"

Vledder growled something unintelligible. His face was still pale.

"If I can't keep it up, I'll park and you can drive the rest of the way."

"Does it hurt?"

Vledder closed his eyes for a split second and groaned.

"Only in the pit of my stomach—now and then I'm nauseous. That guy had a hard head." He shook his head. "My fault, I should have anticipated him. He was getting much too agitated."

DeKok nodded agreement.

"Lucky you fell on your backside, rather than directly on your back. The glass was pretty heavy—good thing it broke into two pieces. Had it shattered we'd be in the hospital now.

Vledder sighed.

"I just got a tear in my jacket."

DeKok grinned.

"With an exhaustive report in triplicate, maybe you'll get reimbursed."

Vledder regained a bit of color.

"I want a new jacket."

"You better forget that. They're not that generous with police funds. Just be glad if they pay for the repair."

Vledder looked stubborn

"I want a new jacket," he repeated petulantly. "No fixing up."

DeKok laughed, relieved. Vledder was getting back to normal.

"You'd be better off suing Jan Rouwen. Just remember, you can't get feathers off a frog."

Even though the analogy was better than the one about bleeding turnips, Vledder was lost in his own thoughts. For a long time he drove on, with clenched teeth and total attention to the road.

After several miles he started the conversation again.

"What do you think?" he asked. "Do you buy Rouwen's story about not knowing what Long Jack wanted to recover from the boardinghouse?"

DeKok grinned.

"Of course he knew. He was bluffing. He knew exactly what Jaap wanted. He wasn't standing around either—he was searching. His prints were on every cupboard and drawer."

"You want to send out an APB for arrest and questioning of those two?"

DeKok shook his head.

"We don't know whether they took anything, or what it might have been. We don't know anything was missing. Can't prove what they were trying to accomplish. All that's left is vandalism, the tearing apart of pillows and mattresses. We can't arrest them for that, especially outside our jurisdiction." He looked out the side window of the car, "At best we can request the location of their domicile. But that's also about all we can do," he added morosely.

Vledder carefully felt his stomach.

"What about assault?"

"Not even that will stick. He did not hit you with intent to maim. He'd had it with us and suddenly wanted to leave. You happened to be in the way."

Vledder swallowed away the nausea.

"You should have been a lawyer," he grunted.

DeKok smiled sadly.

"Maybe I'm a realist. We have a system of law that purports to protect the innocent. But it is the crooks and their lawyers who know how to work the system."

They had reached Amsterdam and moved toward the inner city. By this time the commuters had all left. The rain had driven most of the tourists indoors. The city was quiet. The usual hustle and bustle of Damrak wasn't apparent. Only a handful of pedestrians were to be seen, most of them sprinting for shelter.

Vledder parked the VW around the corner from the station house. Bedraggled, feeling used, the two exited the car. They walked toward the stationhouse by means of Old Bridge Alley.

As they entered the lobby, Kuster, the watch commander, beckoned. They approached him slowly.

"Now what?" asked Vledder.

"There's a dog and pony show upstairs," said Kuster.

"What are you talking about?" asked DeKok.

Kuster raised four fingers in the air.

"Mr. Bavel, his fat cat lawyer, the judge-advocate, and our commissaris are conferring."

DeKok closed his eyes and shook his head as if to clear it. "Why?"

Kuster leaned forward conspiratorially.

"There's been a disappearance—Ramon Bavel."

12

Vledder reacted first.

"You think Waardenburg talked?"

DeKok sighed deeply.

"Looks like it."

Vledder stopped breathing for a moment. The end of his career and life as he knew it swirled in his brain. He pointed to the ceiling.

"The reception committee is especially for me?"

DeKok nodded slowly.

"That's one way of putting it. Sounds more like a tribunal."

Slowly he rubbed the bridge of his nose with a little finger. Then he held the finger up in the air and stared at it, as if he had never seen it before. Then he turned toward Vledder.

"You check into the hospital," he said slowly. "You must be examined, especially your back and stomach. You undoubtedly need x-rays of your spine. You can never be too careful with those things. If they don't keep you there for observation, go home and right to bed. I don't want to see you until tomorrow."

Vledder gave his colleague a long, searching look.

"You're trying to get rid of me."

DeKok smiled.

"I know better than that." He put a hand on the young man's shoulder. "I'm sincere—it would be best to have yourself checked out. That was quite a crash." A boyish grin lit up his face. "The only luck you've had today is no luck at all. Don't make me sorry we came back here, rather than going straight to the hospital." He turned to Kuster. "Could you provide my partner transport?" Kuster nodded and pushed a switch on his desk. DeKok turned and climbed the stairs. With mixed feelings, Vledder watched him go.

Inspector DeKok knocked on the door, immediately opened it, and entered the room. The conversation came to a screeching halt. It took a moment for the occupants to recover.

Then Mr. Schaap allowed a condescending nod of the head. Buitendam, the commissaris, was particularly angry. As he approached DeKok, he gestured toward the corner of the large office, where two men sat in easy chairs.

"This is Mr. Bavel," he said in a condescending voice, "and," pointing at the second man, "this is his legal counsel, Gerard Van Mechelen, Esquire."

DeKok made a formal bow with a courtliness that harkened to the previous century. Meanwhile he tried to place the visitors. Bavel's lawyer had a familiar face. In fact Van Mechelen had demolished DeKok's investigation in a murder case. DeKok had just been transferred to homicide. It was his first, and only, defeat. DeKok remembered the man and his method. The attack had been raw and below the belt, but delivered in a manner DeKok had not been able to counter. The prosecutor was incompetent, which hadn't helped. DeKok developed a wariness from the defeat, always over-preparing for court appearances.

Mr. Bavel was the most sympathetic character in the room. He was a tall, slender man with a sharply delineated face and a touch of gray at the temples. He was expensively dressed in a custom tailored, dark-blue suit. A pure white shirt and pearl-gray necktie completed the ensemble. DeKok estimated Bavel was in his early fifties.

Commissaris Buitendam coughed discreetly.

"These gentlemen," he said pointing at Bavel and his lawyer, "have approached Mr. Schaap, because they are worried. They have asked for an explanation."

DeKok pretended surprise.

"What is it that requires an explanation?"

"Ramon, Mr. Bavel's son, has disappeared."

"I am sorry to hear this. How long has he been missing?"

Mr. Van Mechelen took over the conversation.

"This afternoon. Mr. Bavel had a luncheon appointment with his son at one o'clock this afternoon in the Sonesta Hotel. Mr. Bavel intended to introduce Ramon to some associates. Ramon will be assuming a position in the Mr. Bavel's firm. But Ramon did not appear."

"Then what?"

Mr. Van Mechelen pointed at Mr. Bavel.

"Mr. Bavel found this unsettling. Ramon is extremely punctual. Mr. Bavel called his house. A servant told him that Ramon had left in his car."

"Mrs. Bavel was not at home?"

"She ... eh, she was away, making funeral arrangements for her son, Erik."

DeKok listened intently. He paid particular attention to what was not being said.

"And since that time nobody has seen Ramon?" he asked with a worried look.

If anything Van Mechelen became more patronizing. He opened the lid of his briefcase and produced a sheet of paper. He placed it on the table, but then picked it up again and handed it to DeKok.

"This is what Mr. Bavel found a few hours ago, in his son's room. Perhaps you can explain it?" The tone was now definitely spiteful.

DeKok took the sheet of paper and read out loud: "'The police at Warmoes Street Station intend to arrest me for the murder of Erik and that other boy. It's better that I disappear. Love, Ramon. P. S. Dad, will you take care of this for me?'"

With a grin DeKok returned the sheet of paper.

"And that's what you're here to accomplish?"

"What?"

"You are 'taking care of this' for Ramon."

Mr. Van Mechelen rose from his chair, indignation in his face and posture.

"In the name of my client I demand an explanation."

DeKok shrugged insultingly.

"Did Ramon commit those murders?"

"Preposterous."

"Then why is he running?"

The lawyer snorted.

"Would you want to be arrested for a crime you didn't commit?"

DeKok shook his head.

"I do not arrest innocent people."

"Do you have any proof, any indications that Ramon had anything to do with the murders?"

"No."

Van Mechelen tapped the paper several times with his nails.

"Then why should Ramon believe you're planning to arrest him?"

DeKok grinned.

"You tell me. Does he have an overactive imagination? Or is guilt driving him? What's eating Ramon ... does he have reason to be afraid of an arrest?"

The lawyer shot DeKok a disgusted look.

"Where are the facts? This is all abstract supposition."

DeKok nodded slowly, winking at the lawyer. The lawyer seemed startled and stared at DeKok as if he did not believe he had actually seen a wink.

"Apparently some abstract supposition, as you put it, compelled Ramon to disappear. We never planned to arrest him. Not yet." DeKok paused and took a deep breath. "Your presence here makes me wonder whether you have information you aren't sharing. It also makes me wonder whether your appearance isn't a clever ploy. A slick lawyer might delay an official investigation by helping a suspect flee."

A prominent vein throbbed on Van Mechelen's forehead. He planted himself in front of DeKok, getting close up and personal. His neck was swollen and bulged over his collar.

"What the hell are you insinuating?" he yelled.

DeKok gave him a measured look. He'd never forgotten his distaste for Van Mechelen's machinations. With an effort he controlled himself.

"Call it what you will," he said calmly. "Believe me my superiors wouldn't take it lightly. In any event we would be remiss not to consider the possibility."

Commissaris Buitendam came between the two men. He was shocked. He stretched out an arm toward the door.

DeKok raised his hands in a defensive gesture.

"Never mind, you don't have to say anything … I'm leaving."

He left the room. None of the occupants saw the jubilant smile on his face.

DeKok looked at Vledder and greeted him with a jovial laugh.

"So, what did they say at the hospital?" he asked. "All the parts still in the right place? No broken bones?"

Vledder was enjoying the benefits of a long, restful night. His eyes were clear, there was a healthy blush in his face, and a spring in his step. He threw his coat in the direction of the peg and sank down in the chair behind his desk.

"Just a few bruises and scrapes on my back. No other damage."

"What about your stomach?"

Vledder waved that away.

"If the pain and nausea persist, I have to go back for a picture. So far, so good—I'm a lot better today." He changed the subject. "If I die, it would be from curiosity. What happened with the reception committee?"

DeKok grinned.

"I don't think they're fans."

"Did you loose your temper again?"

DeKok shrugged.

"Bavel's lawyer, Gerard Van Mechelen, went right for my throat. Ramon left a parting note asserting our intention to arrest him. He went on to say he thought it better to disappear. Van Mechelen demanded an explanation."

Vledder bit his lower lip.

"That has to have come straight from Kiliaan Waardenburg," he said ruefully. "He didn't waste much time."

"He left here looking like a man with a mission."

"You didn't let on?"

DeKok shook his head.

"I didn't see the need. I just turned their arguments against them, going on the offensive. I asked Bavel's lawyer whether Ramon had committed the murders. When he characterized my question as preposterous, I asked why Ramon had disappeared if he was so innocent."

Vledder smiled gleefully.

"Then what?"

"I won't bother you with all the details. When I told him Ramon's disappearance appeared to be a lawyer's trick, he exploded. He blocked my path and, for a moment, I thought he wanted to attack me physically. But Buitendam sent me away."

"He didn't explain?"

"Nope."

Vledder laughed out loud.

"Oh that is perfect—just beautiful." It took a while before his laughter faded. "Seriously what do you think of Ramon's disappearance? You don't think it's proof of guilt? Holland is an enlightened country; we have safeguards to protect the innocent. Why would an innocent party run to avoid questioning?"

DeKok looked pensive.

"Now you sound like a lawyer who ..." He did not finish the sentence. "Forget it," he continued in a different tone of voice. "Right after Erik's death Mrs. Bavel assigned the blame to Ramon. Remember how she raked up the history of Ricky's death, almost in the same breath.

I'm sure she didn't stop with us. She will still be talking about Ramon's reprehensible behavior toward both dead brothers. One alarming phone call from either Waardenburg Senior, or Junior, could have created a shock effect ... triggering panic mode."

"You mean that he disappeared *because* he was innocent?"

DeKok nodded firmly.

"You don't have to be the perpetrator to feel guilt. There's such a thing as moral guilt."

"I can't see Ramon burdened with moral guilt? A character like Ramon doesn't suddenly sprout a conscience!" There was disbelief in Vledder's voice.

DeKok raised a cautioning finger in the air.

"Keep in mind we only know Ramon from his mother's description. It wouldn't surprise me to hear exactly the opposite from Pa Bavel." He scratched his ear. "Something keeps telling me there is something wrong in the Bavels' marriage. Pa Bavel made a sympathetic impression on me. If Ramon resembles his father, he may not be the evil, ruthless son his mother portrays. Nonetheless," he added thoughtfully, "there is a peculiar contrast in the parents' behavior. It seems the father was arranging a business lunch for Ramon, while the mother was arranging Erik's funeral."

Vledder nodded in agreement.

"All right," he said after a long pause. "Let's scratch Ramon as a suspect."

DeKok was irritated.

"You go from one extreme to another. Ramon's motives, the ones you attributed to him, have not disappeared with him. Not that his disappearance hasn't added an unnatural emphasis. What I can't choke down is Ramon's involvement in the murder of Jean-Paul. That's quite a stretch. It may be best to avoid taking pot shots—the wrong people could get hurt." A smile curled around his lips. "This is especially true with my old friend, Van Mechelen, in the picture."

He moved in his chair and shook his head.

"We have virtually no case, do you realize that?"

"How do you mean? We have two corpses."

"Exactly and that's about all we have. We have one crime scene that consists of some bricks near the canal. The area has been washed clean several times by the rain. The other crime scene has been vandalized by our friends from Utrecht." He changed his tone. "I still can't believe Mina Lyons ignored the police tape on the doors and showed the room to new boarders," he mused. Then he continued more vigorously: "But put that aside. No crime scenes, as I said. We have no suspects worth mentioning, because we have decided the same individual committed both murders. Above all, we have no solid motive. As I said," he concluded, "we have two corpses."

He glanced at the clock on the wall.

"The two boys will be buried at eleven this morning at West Gardens. Why don't you have a look and see who attends the services. You have to be there anyway to inspect the coffins."

He stood up and took his hat and coat from the peg. Vledder followed him.

"And you? What are you going to do?"

"I'm going to have a cup of coffee with an old friend."

"Who?"

"Handie Henkie," replied DeKok with a wide grin.

13

___

Handie Henkie, the ex-burglar looked at DeKok with suspicious eyes. He tilted his head, as if to get a better look.

"Did you really come to see me, just to have a cup of coffee?" He sounded skeptical. "Somehow I find that hard to believe. You're up to something."

"How is your daughter?"

"Excellent."

"No more problems?"

"No."

"It's been a while since I've seen her."

Henkie slapped his hand on the table.

"Come on, DeKok," he said with annoyance, "quit stalling. What do you want?"

DeKok lowered his eyes and scratched the back of his head.

"Well," he began, "not to put too fine a point on it, I wanted ... I want you to come with me. His tone was hesitant. "I don't think I can manage on my own."

The ex-burglar shook his head resolutely.

"Nothing doing," he declared firmly. "Forget about it! I won't do it anymore. During that last trip you asked me to help you, so much went wrong that I was glad to get out of it with my skin intact. I swore I would *never* do it again. I just don't want to run the risk. Why should I?"

He looked at DeKok. "Do you know how long I've been a free man?"

DeKok nodded slowly.

"Seventeen years, eight months, three weeks, and ... eh, two days."

Handie Henkie looked surprised.

"You've been keeping track?"

DeKok was serious.

"Just before I came over, I looked up your record."

"Why?"

"Because, I just wanted to know."

Henkie lost his temper. He gesticulated wildly.

"I'm doing very well, DeKok. No problems. I live in a nice apartment. I wouldn't like to trade it for a cell."

DeKok nodded his understanding.

"On the way here, I thought about it." His voice was sad. "I realized that I had called on you too often. I knew it had to come to an end sooner or later."

Henkie grinned.

"Are you getting all sentimental on me, is that it?"

DeKok stroked his gray hair.

"Why not. Haven't I known you for a quarter century? That is a large chunk out of a person's life. In the beginning I was out to get you. I even presented you with a couple of years in jail. Even so, you were always ready to help me. You don't forget things like that, Henkie. You keep that in your heart."

The old burglar moved restlessly in his chair.

"Cut out the soft soap, DeKok," he said crustily. "I'm not going to let you persuade me. I'm not hitting the bricks with you and that's final." He sighed deeply. His tone became milder. "Besides, times have changed. Nothing is like it used to be." He gestured with both hands. "What do I know about modern security methods with all that electronics stuff? Nothing. I know about locks. I know how to open a safe. That was all you needed in my day."

DeKok pointed at his host.

"According to me, you're still the greatest burglar of all time in the eastern hemisphere."

"You mean the western hemisphere," said Henkie peevishly.

"No, that's what most people think, because we're in western Europe. But we're actually in the eastern hemisphere. Look it up in an atlas."

"It's all the same to me."

"Well, it doesn't really matter," admitted DeKok. "Either way, you're probably the best in *both* hemispheres."

Handie Henkie shook his head.

"Don't start again. You know where I stand."

DeKok smiled.

"I thought you were going to serve coffee."

"Anything new from West Garden?"

Vledder shrugged.

"Just the morbid curiosity of professional mourners. Other than that I met the family of Jean-Paul Stappert for the first time ... his mother. She came from Paris. That's where she lives now."

"And his father?"

Vledder shook his head.

"Not on paper—the "birth" father was a very seductive French musician. He and Suzanne Stappert lived together for a few years. In her youth she went to Paris to learn

French, made her living as an au-pair. She met the musician at a party given by her employers. According to Mother Stappert it was love at first sight."

DeKok grimaced.

"She should have looked twice."

Vledder ignored the remark and continued stolidly.

"They lived together in rented rooms in the Latin Quarter, close to the Sorbonne. They lived well and enthusiastically."

"You made that up."

"Sort of, but that was the gist of her comments."

"But that ended when little Jean-Paul presented himself."

Vledder nodded.

"Exactly. The vivacious and apparently, virile musician, literally vanished into the night. Suzanne went back to Amsterdam to deliver her baby. She registered the infant under her name, since there was no marriage. Suzanne worked long, hard years for her child and she made sure that Jean-Paul, who was named after his father, finished high school. A few months after getting his diploma, he became addicted to heroin. She tried everything to get him into rehabilitation. When she was unable to help him, she could no longer watch her son sink into a morass of misery. She fled to Paris—where she had once been happy."

DeKok looked absent-minded.

"She told you all that? It sounds like a cheap melo-drama."

Vledder nodded sadly.

"True," he said, "But that is her story. She confided it to me in a bar near the railroad station. There were a few hours to wait before her train left."

"How did you get to know her?"

"I happened to see her write her name in the guest book of the chapel and I introduced myself." Vledder stared into the distance with a vague smile on his lips. "Suzanne is a striking woman. She makes an impression—very intelligent and still quite attractive. I took her to the station and just before the train left she gave me a very sensual kiss."

DeKok frowned.

"It doesn't look like her son's death left much of an impression."

"There's an explanation," answered Vledder. "For her, he died five years ago, when she said goodbye and left for Paris."

DeKok twiddled his fingers.

"Did she have any theories about her son's mysterious death? Her greatest fear might have been losing him to an overdose. Drugs did not kill him as she expected ... he was killed in cold blood." He paused for an answer. But when that was not forthcoming, he added: "You did tell her under what circumstances Jean-Paul came to his end?"

"Certainly."

"And?"

Vledder hesitated.

"She ... she didn't give the means of his death much weight," he said slowly. "As far as she was concerned, murder was just one more facet of life. Not much different than dying in an accident, or because of some illness."

"And you agree with that?"

Vledder shrugged.

"She was right about one thing—the result is always the same ... death."

DeKok snorted.

"How many glasses of cognac did you drink while you were waiting for her train?"

"Two, three ..." grinned Vledder.

"Maybe you lost count?"

Vledder shook his head.

"No, really. No more than three. But she captivated me while I drank them. Under different circumstances ... with a little more time ... I might have fallen in love."

DeKok analyzed the expression on his colleague's face—the vague smile, the dreamy look in his blue eyes.

"I'm even prepared to believe that," he sighed. He snapped his fingers under Vledder's nose to wake him from his reverie. "Did you see Pa Bavel at the funeral?"

It took a few seconds. Then the vague smile disappeared and Vledder looked more like the alert policeman he was. He shook his head.

"He didn't make an appearance. At least Mrs. Bavel wasn't with him. And I didn't see anybody who looked like your description of the man. Mother Bavel was accompanied by a woman. I thought it might be a sister, there was some resemblance." He paused before he continued. "I secretly hoped Ramon might show up."

"But he wasn't there?"

"He wasn't there," agreed Vledder.

"Would you have recognized him?"

"Sure. Before I went to West Garden I called my buddy in Heemstede. He gave me a detailed description."

"Did he know Ramon has disappeared?"

"Yes, Pa Bavel reported it to the Heemstede police, accompanied by his lawyer. They filed an official missing person report, so the police can put things in motion."

"And what did the Heemstede police do?"

"Well, according to my buddy, the police there saw no reason to assume that Ramon was a missing person.

According to the law, Ramon is an adult, who disappeared on his own accord. Absent any evidence of an accident, the person must have been missing for at least seventy-two hours, before the police can act. Nothing would lead them to believe he was harmed or kidnapped."

DeKok rubbed his chin.

"I can't help wondering what sort of game Gerard Van Mechelen, Esquire, is playing. He must have known that a missing person report was ludicrous under the circumstances. He's after an effect."

"How is that?"

"Say the Heemstede police take the report at face value. They send out an APB and initiate the official search. Van Mechelen produces Ramon's letter. In the letter he points the finger at us—says we're going to arrest him. Bam! Internal affairs is on the case. Instead of investigating the murders, we're up to our necks just trying to defend ourselves and each other. It's quite possible, you know, we're off the case altogether. The Department of Justice has little tolerance for even a suspected transgression by one of us."

Vledder chewed his lower lip, deep in thought.

"It would probably get us off the case," he admitted after a long silence. "Perhaps Van Mechelen is trying to get even with us for some perceived slight. I'm not so sure he's driven by resentment. Perhaps he thinks Ramon *might* have committed the murders."

DeKok thought about that.

"If Ramon had been at the funeral this morning, would you have arrested him?"

Vledder's face froze.

"Absolutely," he said. "He'd be in custody, even if I had to pull him from his brother's graveside."

DeKok shook his head in disapproval.

"One should never interrupt the ceremonies surrounding birth, matrimony, and death," he said mildly. "Not even with the law on your side."

The phone rang. Vledder picked it up. His face fell ashen as he replaced the receiver with a shaking hand.

"Mina, Mina Lyons," he gasped.

"Dead?" asked DeKok.

"Murdered," nodded Vledder.

14

The rooming house keeper was supine, almost in the center of the spotless, white-marble kitchen floor. The outstretched left arm was at a ninety degrees angle from the body and ended in a clawed hand. Her well-shaped legs were slightly spread and her bare feet were covered with the ugly slippers.

Sadness overcame DeKok as he surveyed the body of the dead woman. His sharp eyes went from the slippers along the faded red housecoat to the sharp face with its tawny skin. He looked at the long, black hair spread out on the cold marble floor, the broken eyes, the half open mouth, the streaked make-up.

He took it all in and, without conscious effort, stored the details in his uniquely photographic memory. He'd honed his ability to recall detail over the years. He pushed his old, decrepit hat a bit back on his head and scratched his forehead. He was disquieted—something didn't fit. He'd developed another skill over long years of training and experience. One of the first things he looked for was the anomaly; it was like listening for dissonance. Even the tiniest detail out of place at the scene of a murder jumped out at him. In this case, the corpse itself was out of place in the spotless kitchen. DeKok sensed something less obvious, but not readily apparent.

Vledder knelt next to the head of the deceased and looked closely at the neck.

"Strangled," he said evenly.

DeKok nodded vaguely. His discomfort was growing. He found it difficult to tear his attention away from the corpse. What could he be missing?

Vledder rose to his feet.

"She didn't deserve this," he said somberly. "No, she did not deserve to die like this."

DeKok grimaced.

"Somebody thought she did."

Vledder used a handkerchief to wipe the sweat off his brow. He did not have as much experience as his partner. He was always upset when confronted with violent death. DeKok had often assured him he always would be. Over the years he would simply learn to hide it better.

"Murderers," observed Vledder, "are strange people."

"Rarely," answered DeKok, still staring at the corpse. "They are almost always frighteningly average."

Vledder pointed at the dead woman.

"The strangulation marks," he said, "are about identical to those on the boys. The autopsy will determine that definitely, but I'm willing to bet on it."

DeKok sighed deeply.

Vledder's face suddenly turned red. With an angry gesture he pointed around the kitchen.

"For heaven's sake, DeKok," he exclaimed, "why?" He bit his lower lip. "She was no friend of mine. My only meeting with her was as unpleasant as she could make it. But she was a hardworking woman who tried to make an honest living."

"Perhaps."

Vledder looked startled.

"Oh no?" he queried. He waved around. His young face was mottled. "Do you see any wealth? Her kitchen is bare ... sterile like an operating theater. I looked in her living room. It's also spotless, but sparsely furnished ... with a few threadbare pieces. A blind horse could do no damage there."

"What's your point?"

Vledder snorted.

"If she was a criminal, where's the money?"

DeKok looked pensive.

"Crime ... is not always profitable."

Bram Weelen, DeKok's favorite police photographer entered. He smiled at Vledder, then, at DeKok.

"Are you turning over a new leaf?"

"What?" asked DeKok, still fully focused on the corpse.

Weelen put down his heavy equipment case.

"It's still daylight," he said, brightly. "The sun is shining. We usually get summoned in the middle of the night."

DeKok pointed at the dead woman.

"We've only known for about fifteen minutes. One of her guests was checking on his mail and found her body. She's been dead, I think, since last night."

"Strangled?"

"Yes."

"Like the two boys?"

DeKok nodded.

"There are some similarities."

Weelen shook his head.

"So, what is it with this boardinghouse?"

DeKok gave him a wan smile.

"If I knew that maybe we could keep anyone else from being victimized, at least, here."

"Why don't you evacuate everybody? Get 'em out and board it up. End of problem."

DeKok shook his head.

"We'd have to get the building condemned ... under what pretense?"

Weelen lifted his aluminum suitcase on the counter next to the sink.

"How should I know?" he growled. "You guys are the heroes. I just take the pictures."

The old inspector finally turned away from the corpse. In the door opening stood Dr. Koning, the eccentric coroner. Behind him in the corridor was his whole entourage of morgue attendants with a collapsible stretcher and the body bag.

DeKok welcomed the doctor and shook his hand. He liked the old man very much. The two of them formed a sort of tragic-comedic duo, too often confronting violent death.

Dr. Koning lifted his old-fashioned Garibaldi hat and pointed at the corpse.

"Busy days, busy days," he murmured, shaking his head. He looked at DeKok, "Wretched weather affects people, you know ... it's been scientifically established. In Switzerland murder, suicide, and deadly accidents increase during a foehn—hence the term Foehn Disease. It seems the sudden rise in temperature, combined with the wind, creates a ..." He stopped when he saw DeKok smile politely. "I know," added the doctor, "sometimes I rattle on. Well," he continued briskly, "let's see what we have here."

Dr. Koning knelt down next to the dead woman, felt

her cheek with the back of his hand and looked at the strangulation marks on the neck. He crawled backward and removed one of the ugly slippers to feel a foot. His old knees creaked as he rose.

"I, eh," hesitated DeKok, "think it may have happened last night. She's stiff and she feels cold."

Dr. Koning looked at him.

"You know I don't like to make observations before the autopsy," he censored. "But in this case, you may very well be right. Rigor mortis is complete." He shook his head. "But I would not depend too much on the body temperature. The cold, marble floor drains all body heat very quickly." He pursed his lips. "Just an estimate—the time of death was approximately eight to ten hours ago. Not much earlier."

DeKok was shocked.

"So … this took place sometime in the wee hours this morning."

Dr. Koning produced an old fashioned watch from his vest pocket and consulted it. Then he put it back with precise gestures and made sure the watch chain was where it was supposed to be.

"Indeed," he confirmed, "early this morning. Again this was done with bare hands. Your murderer has strong hands and a very powerful grip—maybe, a tennis player." He took off his pince-nez and, then, looked through it from about a foot away. "We talked about this possibility before."

DeKok nodded calmly.

"Yes, after the death of that boy, upstairs. And later … when we found the boy at Emperor's Canal."

The coroner studied DeKok for at least ten seconds

through his hand-held glasses. Then he replaced them on his nose and replaced his big hat. He waved at Vledder and started to leave the kitchen. As he approached the door, he hesitated, then turned around and pointed at the corpse.

"Oh, and, she *is* dead," he said. It sounded cynical.

Bram Weelen hunkered down with his Hasselblad in his hands. He started his first series of pictures from close to the ground. When the lights flashed for the third time, Kruger, the fingerprint expert entered. He was huffing and puffing. His face was haggard.

DeKok gave him a searching look.

"Been in a fight?"

Kruger slammed his case down next to that of Weelen.

"I've done four burglaries, a robbery, and a disguised suicide today. The day isn't over yet, but I'm ready to chuck it in."

DeKok pointed at the surroundings.

"According to Vledder this is a sterile kitchen. You won't find anything."

"Anything from the herd?" asked Kruger. The dactyloscopist knew DeKok's terminology. He also compared the small army that gathered at murder scenes to Woody Herman's band.

"Not yet," said DeKok. He made it a policy to leave before the "herd". The professional crime scene investigators, supplied by headquarters, served their purpose. It was the chief inspectors and higher authorities that accompanied them who were useless. Even the judge-advocate would send at least one representative. DeKok preferred to work with what he called his "own" team of experts. He had worked with Kruger and Weelen for years and knew them as capable and cooperative professionals. He included Vledder as a matter of course. In DeKok's opinion, that was all he needed. The CSI people could save him and Vledder some time-consuming legwork. DeKok preferred his own, sometimes unorthodox, methods of investigation. Until now he had been very successful.

Vledder walked over.

"You seemed surprised when Dr. Koning told you she'd been dead for only eight or ten hours. Why is it strange that she was killed early this morning, instead of last night?"

DeKok pointed at the corpse.

"The make-up," he said. "I've known Mina Lyons for years and I've seen her countless times. Mina wasn't a woman who used make-up early in the day. Her skin was her best feature—she wore no make-up at all."

Vledder shrugged.

"Perhaps she was expecting a visitor and she wanted to look good."

DeKok nodded morosely.

"Yes, Dick, sometimes you make very pertinent observations."

DeKok had tired feet. With a contorted face he placed both legs on top of his desk. A hellish pain started in his toes and spread the length of his legs. It felt as if a thousand small devils penetrated his muscles with tiny, red-hot pitchforks.

The excruciating sensation affected his mood. He knew what it meant, knew it was completely psychosomatic. No physical cause had ever been diagnosed. The pain always, and only, appeared on certain occasions. It returned when he was in the middle of a case and saw no solution. Just now he had not even a hint of a solution.

He shook his head to clear it. We're in a dead end, he reflected. The death of Mina Lyons blind-sided him. He saw no way to fit it into the tenuous pattern he'd been developing.

The manner of death was strikingly similar in the case of the boys. There was no doubt about that. But if Mina was involved ... how? Why would the killer want her dead? Why wait five days? Was there a closer relationship between Mina Lyons and the boys than just landlord and lodger? If so what sort of relationship could they have had?

No matter how he tortured his brain, he could not find a connecting point, let alone a solution. And the little devils in his legs continued their piercing dance. He leaned forward, pulled his pants legs over his knees, and rubbed both legs vigorously. It gave a brief, momentary relief.

Vledder also knew the symptoms and looked concerned.

"Tired feet?" he asked anxiously. Although the pain spread through the entire legs, DeKok always referred to it as "tired feet."

DeKok nodded agreement.

"Yes, I would like to have Jan Veldstra here right now."

"Who's Veldstra?"

"My doctor. He doesn't believe me about the leg pain. Just imagination, he claims."

Vledder looked doubtful.

"And what does the doctor say when somebody has died?"

DeKok gave a crooked grin.

"Yes, he probably tells the patient, 'don't worry, it's all in your head!'"

Suddenly he laughed out loud. It was a reaction to his own cynicism. Then the pain drained away as suddenly as it had appeared. With renewed energy he pulled down his pants legs and started to pace up and down the busy detective room. The cadence helped him to order his thoughts.

There had to be a way to bring order out of the chaos. For one thing how did Alex Waardenburg, the music teacher, and his son, Kiliaan, fit into the picture? Were they involved in the murders of the two boys, or were they just on the periphery? Why did Ramon disappear? Why were Pa Bavel and his pricey lawyer so intent on impeding the murder investigation? Was Bavel motivated by fear? Fear for the guilt of his son?

The next puzzle piece was the involvement of Jaap Santen and Jan Rouwen, the punks from Utrecht. Did they act on their own initiative, or were they used by someone? Perhaps Willy Haarveld, the eccentric, self-proclaimed impresario had manipulated them?

DeKok pondered whether those were the only players in this sinister game of death? Or were there others yet undiscovered? Were there any more targets out there? Above all what drove this murderer?

Who would want the two boys dead—who would profit? Not to mention what was the commonality with, of all people, Mina Lyons?

He continued to pace. Were these the only questions? If he had the answers, could he solve the cases? Even though he could be dealing with three separate motives, he felt there was more to understand about the boardinghouse keeper and her boarders.

In a subconscious reaction he avoided Adjutant Jong as he entered the room. He approached Vledder's desk, just as another officer handed his partner a flimsy piece of paper. It was a fax message. DeKok couldn't help giving in to his curiosity. He moved to Vledder's side.

"Something special?"

Vledder looked up from the message.

"Jaap Santen has been arrested."

"Where?"

"In Antwerp, with six pounds of heroin."

15

Vledder pushed the keyboard of his computer aside.

"You want me to go to Antwerp?"

"To do what?"

"I could interrogate Santen. I'm sure a colleague from narcotics will be glad to come as well. The Belgian police will cooperate. I know that."

DeKok thought for a moment.

"You'll need permission from the judge-advocate to cross the border. And will he give it? I don't know. The only thing we got on Santen is vandalism. I just don't think they will allow the funds for a trip to Belgium on something as flimsy as that."

Vledder leaned forward.

"I checked with narcotics. They've had Santen under observation for months. It seems Long Jack is a smuggler. He gets most of the coke and H that is consumed in and around Utrecht into the country."

"So, how did he come to be arrested?"

"Headquarters received an anonymous tip that Long Jack had left for Antwerp by car. He was supposed to meet a ship and receive a quantity of drugs. The tipster described the auto, right down to the color, make, model, tag number, and year. Get this—the car had been stolen in Utrecht. The cop at headquarters, Jagerman, signaled Antwerp to alert them. Two Belgian cops were waiting for Long Jack when he came off the ship."

"Jagerman … is that Ed Jagerman?"

"Yes."

"I know him. Is he aware of our interest?"

"Well, of course, he knew we were working on a couple of murders. He knew we had asked for the location of Santen and Rouwen. That's why he forwarded the message from Antwerp."

DeKok nodded to himself.

"Does Jagerman know about any connection between Santen and Erik Bavel … perhaps in combination with Jean-Paul?"

Vledder shook his head.

"No, I mentioned the names. But Jagerman only knows them as users. That's all. Mina Lyons was a complete unknown to him. He'd never heard her name in connection with the drug trade."

"Who was going to take care of the distribution?"

"What distribution?"

"Oh, come on," said DeKok impatiently. "Who distributed the drugs Santen brought in?"

"I didn't ask."

DeKok grinned.

"It would be best to do so. We're much too parochial in our approach to crime. Other divisions may very well have information we can use. We need to know everything narcotics can tell us. "I worry," he added reflectively, "we all focus on our own problems. There isn't enough reciprocation between departments."

"The computer network is supposed to take care of that," said Vledder.

"Computers," said DeKok. He said it as if it were a dirty word. "Anyway, check up on the possible distributor, although I have a good idea whose name will pop up."

Vledder was going to defend the computers some more, when his face suddenly lit up.

"Of course," he exclaimed, "Willy ... Willy Haarveld! He lives close to Utrecht. He's connected in the performing arts. He knows performers, promoters, producers, the television stations in Hilversum, you name it. God! It's as clear as Erik Bavel's eyes."

DeKok laughed.

"And who do you think might have been the anonymous caller?"

"Jagerman's snitch?"

"Who else?"

Vledder hesitated.

"Haarveld again?" he tried cautiously.

DeKok nodded approval.

"It wouldn't be a surprise. Whoever it was had unusual details: the location of the transaction, the exact description of the car. Few people in Santen's environment would be in a position to know all that."

"Say it was Willy. Why would he want to destroy his own supply line?"

DeKok waved that away with a nonchalant gesture.

"It's not a matter of destroying a source, that can be reconstructed. The purpose is to destroy Long Jack." He paused and took a deep breath. "I think, after our visit to Santen's place, Jan Rouwen contacted Haarveld immediately. Our slick friend drew his own conclusions. Our interest in Long Jack would have worried him."

"And Santen became excess baggage?"

"Why else?"

"Santen would divert us?"

"Certainly. Look at it from Haarveld's point of view. He has no idea where our investigations have led us … he has no idea if we know anything about his drug dealing. Jaap Santen could be an embarrassing witness." he grinned maliciously. "Much better to have him picked up in Antwerp. He'd be convicted there, probably would do jail time."

"But Santen could decide to talk at any time."

"Not so easy from a Belgian jail," smiled DeKok. "It's speculative, I admit. Perhaps Willy Haarveld didn't think it all the way through. If he was feeling the heat he might have just wanted to get his courier out of the way for a time." He narrowed his eyes. "What if Ed Jagerman had followed a different tactic?"

"What different tactic?"

"Instead of alerting the Belgian police he could have let Santen come home. He could have followed him until Santen delivered the goods."

Vledder slapped his hand on the desk.

"Haarveld would have been in deep trouble."

DeKok pointed a finger at his friend.

"You see? That's why the tip was so complete. Narcotics had to react. The bait was so enticing."

Vledder sank back in his chair and scratched the back of his neck. DeKok's theories washed over him. It seemed like a long time before he spoke again.

"So, Mina Lyons could have been right," he opined. "Long Jack and Rouwen *could* have been looking for dope. The murder of both boys could be tracked to people in the drug trade."

DeKok did not answer at once. He felt exhausted all of a sudden. He sighed.

"And why was Mina Lyons killed?" he asked wanly. "It wasn't what she did, it was what she knew. Someone wanted to silence her. She was a liability for the same reason Santen was a liability to Haarveld."

"And who could have committed her murder?" asked Vledder. Then he answered his own question: "Jan Rouwen."

The club Little Lowee liked to call his "establishment" was near the corner of Barn Alley and Rear Fort Canal. DeKok stepped through the curtains in the entryway. The intimate bar was always poorly lit.

At a small table in a corner two old ladies were seated, drinking their schnapps. The retired prostitutes looked like anyone's vision of the perfect grandmother. They turned and raised their glasses in greeting. Nobody was seated at the bar.

DeKok ambled to the bar and hoisted himself on the far stool, his back against the wall.

Little Lowee wiped his hands on his greasy vest and greeted DeKok with a broad smile.

"I never seen you this early before," he said cheerfully "Nuttinn doin at your place, eh?" He dived under the bar and held up a bottle of cognac. "Too early?"

DeKok shook his head.

"No," he said, "it'll be good medicine. I can't shake the blues."

Little Lowee looked concerned.

"Ain't gettin anywheres?"

DeKok shook his head as he watched Lowee pour.

"It's crazy," he admitted, "but I seem to be just as far as in the beginning. Nowhere."

"I heard they done in Mina too."

DeKok sighed deeply.

"Just as I was getting hopeful about solving the two murders, a boarder finds Mina dead. It changed everything—takes me back to square one. What a mess."

Lowee pushed the glass closer to the detective. For himself he poured a cup of coffee, although, with a generous measure of cognac.

"Gotta watch it," he said apologetically. "Can't start too early, or I goes to da floor before closing time. Where's your mate, then?"

"My mate," he smiled, "took the train for Antwerp this morning. They arrested someone there who is a person of interest in the murders."

"I knows 'im?"

"Are you curious?"

The small barkeeper spread his hands.

"Maybe I can sorta help you. You never knows. I gotta a contact here and there."

"Jaap Santen."

Lowee snorted.

"Knows 'im as Skinny Jack. He's a filthy little rat—wouldn't stop at nuttin."

"Do you think he'd be capable of murder?"

Lowee nodded with emphasis.

"Yep, yessir. He had a sorta pal. Jan van Utrecht, another loser."

"Jan van Utrecht?"

"Yep that's what they calls him, 'cause he's from Utrecht. His real moniker is Rouwen."

DeKok took a careful sip from the cognac. He did not seem to savor it as he usually did. It was just a sip. It could have been water.

"Are you good at music?"

Lowee did not understand the question.

"Music ... whadda youse mean?"

DeKok replaced his glass on the counter and leaned closer.

"Last time you told me that Jean-Paul Stappert—Mr. Melody to you—played music on half filled glasses."

"Yep."

"I had the idea he only did that once."

Lowee shook his head.

"Nah, it turned into a sorta game. In da end, I kept them glasses the way he done filled 'em on da shelf. Good for business."

"I don't understand that."

Lowee's small face beamed.

"There was lotsa people in the joint. He plays somethin' on them glasses. Lotsa people like it and stay. Then they orders some more and listen some more, youse know."

"And he always played something different?"

Lowee nodded.

"Yep, always new stuff, too."

"Do you remember any melodies?"

Lowee thought hard.

"Nah," he said finally, "they ain't in my head. Yeah ... if I hears 'em again, then ..." He did not complete the sentence. "Nevermind—lotsa people come back all atime 'cause he's gonna play. They was real fans, you knows."

DeKok lifted his glass again and drank in silence.

"Can you give me a list?" he asked as he drained his glass.

"What sorta list?"

"A list of names, names of people who came to hear Mr. Melody's music. The fans."

Lowee looked suspicious.

"Whadda want wid 'em? I don't wanna lose customers to the cops."

DeKok made a helpless gesture.

"You won't. I'm not sure yet why I want the list … really I don't, Lowee. But I promise that I won't use the list until I talk to you first."

The barkeeper hesitated a moment longer.

"Okay then," he said. He pointed at the glass and asked: "Want another one?"

DeKok shook his head.

"No, Lowee, you were right, it is too early. But the first did its work. It got rid of the cobwebs."

"How's about a cuppa coffee, then?"

"That would be welcome … but without the improvements."

"Nah, those is only for barkeeps."

He poured the coffee and placed the cup in front of DeKok as he removed the empty glass.

"How long has Willy Haarveld been dealing drugs?" asked DeKok casually.

Little Lowee gave him a blank stare.

"How long he do wha'?"

DeKok laughed out loud.

"You don't know?"

Lowee raised his hands over his head.

"Lissen, DeKok," he said seriously. "I don't mind picking up something now and again. A stand up guy comes in here and has intel, I wanna make a buck, just like the next guy.

But some street scum comes in here talkin' coke, big H …
nossir, I don't want to know."

DeKok gave him a friendly nod.

"If you did I would never darken your door again."

"Well that proves it, then. I wouldn't wanna loose my
best customer."

DeKok sipped his coffee, while Lowee rinsed some
glasses. Then he came back to where DeKok was sitting.

"You knows who was here this week?"

"Well?"

"Handie Henkie."

"What did Handie have to say for himself?"

Lowee nodded slowly.

"He just say he were sorry."

DeKok drained his coffee cup and looked at the small
barkeeper with a thoughtful look. He slid off the stool and
left the bar with a smile on his lips.

16

By his own admission, DeKok was the worst driver in all the Netherlands, possibly all of Europe. But with Vledder in Antwerp, he had no choice. That is why he was on the road to Amersfoort, which is situated just west of Utrecht. The dented, much abused, VW Beetle assigned to the Warmoes Street Homicide team groaned under the torture of DeKok's lead foot, abrupt clutching, and gear popping.

It was a stretch to call this driving. He was unfamiliar with the route, but impatient. It was more man versus machine, as DeKok prodded the recalcitrant bug. Once again, he reflected briefly on the disadvantages of driving oneself. It was too distracting, he thought. He liked to sit back and view the scenery while he let his thoughts roam. Now he had to pay constant attention to what he was doing and he considered it an annoying imposition. He longed for the times when traffic moved behind a horse-drawn coach or canal barge.

He held the steering wheel in a death grip while his eyes stayed on the road ahead. He could not relax, didn't dare let his eyes wander to the mirrors, or anywhere outside his lane of traffic. With this narrow-angle vision he was constantly surprised by passing traffic. He'd never quite learned the trick of keeping an intermittent eye on the rearview mirror.

"Why did you change your mind?" he asked Henkie, without taking his eyes off the road.

"Not because of you," answered Handie Henkie. He held on to the strap over his head with one hand and braced himself against the dashboard with the other.

"Oh," replied DeKok, "I thought it was because of our long acquaintance."

"You're the one who convinced me, years ago, to give up my life of crime," said Henkie heatedly. "It wasn't bad advice. I'm much better off now. I make more money than as a burglar. But I've grown proud of being a solid citizen. I've obeyed the law, except for the times you've asked me to bend it—like now. It doesn't set well."

"It's in the interest of justice, never for gain," said DeKok as reasonably as possible between clenched teeth. "You know it isn't about money or vengeance."

Handie Hankie shifted his grip slightly.

"Your justice ain't necessarily mine. I mean, it's your job. You're being paid to take certain risks because of what you call justice. I don't."

"Fair enough. But I still don't know why you changed your mind."

"Because of Mina."

DeKok almost dared give Henkie a surprised look, but then thought better of it. He kept his eyes on the road.

"Mina Lyons?"

"Yes. When I read in the paper that they had killed her, I went to see Little Lowee to get the details. Lowee always knows everything. He for sure knows a lot more than you read in the paper. He told me Mina's death was connected somehow with the other two murders and *that's* when I decided to help you."

"Because of Mina?"

Henkie lowered his head, but DeKok did not see it.

"I've known her since forever. She used to help me when I was still working in my former ... eh, profession. She never minded hiding loot for a few days, or a few months, if necessary. I could use her place as a hideout anytime, if the police was a little close on my heels."

"You never told me that."

"Why should I? It was between Mina and me. Please understand. There was never anything between us, no romance. She had her johns and, later, a husband. She was just a great friend with a heart to help." He sighed deeply. "The bastard who strangled her needs to choke to death." He paused. "Well, I mean ... sentenced to hang. It galls me to think of him free to live his life."

DeKok smiled.

"So, my justice, after all."

"Forget you," said Henkie and then he added: "Better yet, why don't you pull over and let me drive. We'd have a shot at arriving in one piece."

"It's a police car," said DeKok.

"So what. It's unmarked and it would be safer."

With a grateful sigh, DeKok aimed the much abused vehicle to the side of the road. They changed seats and as DeKok sank down in the passenger seat, Handie Henkie smoothly shifted up and resumed their journey.

Soon they reached "het Gooi," a picturesque strip of heather and pine forests. It lies between Amsterdam and Utrecht. The Dutch radio and television industry is located there, in the city of Hilversum. Holland is so small, all the transmitters located around Hilversum easily cover Holland, as well as large areas of Belgium, Germany, and the coastal regions of England. After the strip between The Hague and Haarlem, which includes the cities of Wassenaar and Heemstede/Aerdenhout, "het Gooi" is the second most prosperous part of the country.

Before reaching Amersfoort, they turned off toward Laren. The city was asleep. Soon they reached Zevender Drift, a well kempt lane, bordered by wide grass strips and stately old trees. The gardens overflowed with rhododendrons.

"This it?" asked Henkie.

"Yes," answered DeKok. "Just a few more houses, on the right."

Henkie passed the house and parked the Beetle under some trees.

They exited the car and Henkie locked it, after taking a bag from the back seat. Then he gave the keys back to DeKok. Silently they walked back on the grass.

They stopped in front of a wide driveway, marked by two antique streetlights. Henkie pointed at the house.

"Anybody home?"

DeKok shook his head.

"The owner is Willy Haarveld. He's a music pro-ducer—calls himself an impresario. The orchestra he has under contract is giving a farewell performance in Arnhem, Afterwards there's a party. He won't be back before at least two in the morning."

Handie Henkie glanced at his watch.

"That gives us just three quarters of an hour."

DeKok grinned boyishly.

"It's plenty of time for someone with your skills."

They approached the house.

"What are we after?" whispered Henkie.

DeKok shrugged in the darkness.

"I don't know ... not exactly ... a motive for the killing of two boys ... and Mina."

"Brought to you by the Department of Planning," sputtered Henkie. "With this strategy I could be a three-time loser and you could be without a badge."

They walked around the villa. In the back Henkie pointed at a window, partly ajar.

"Bingo," he whispered. "This won't take long. Go to the front door and I'll let you in as if you were announced."

DeKok ambled away and sniffed the air. It was a sultry night and the aroma of flowers was invigorating. He was completely at ease, no qualms. Instead he felt a sort of resigned acceptance. He smiled thinking what might have been had fate dealt him a different hand. He and Henkie would have made a terrific criminal duo. The idea amused him.

When he arrived at the front door, the ex-burglar was waiting for him with an inviting gesture.

"I don't think you need me," said Henkie in a normal tone of voice. "I haven't seen a safe yet."

"Perhaps it's a wall safe, hidden behind a painting."

"Paintings," snorted Henkie. "This guy has some weird taste. The white and purple walls are bare. Everything is white or purple, even the canopy bed in the bedroom."

"You've been there already?"

"Sure, that's where I entered."

DeKok moved the beam of his flashlight around the entrance hall.

"There must be an office."

The ex-burglar nodded in agreement.

"But that will probably be in the front of the house. The living room and bedroom open up to the rear garden."

DeKok looked concerned for a moment.

"Did you leave any traces?" he asked anxiously.

Henkie shook his head.

"You had to ask? No way. After we're finished we leave by the front door and use your little gimmick to lock it nice and tight. Nobody will be the wiser."

"Did you wipe your feet?"

Handie Henkie looked hurt.

"How do you think I got my nickname?" he asked indignantly. "I don't leave no traces. Never have. When you nicked me, it was because of the loot, never because of what you found at the scene. I knew what I was doing and I haven't lost it yet."

DeKok made a soothing sound.

Henkie opened a door to the right of the hall and used his own flashlight. A white painted desk stood in front of a light purple wall. The ex-burglar grinned.

"You see, purple and white ... white and purple."

DeKok entered the room. He tested the drawers of the desk. They were not locked. He opened the upper right hand drawer and rummaged among the papers. Suddenly he spotted a folder with "Jean-Paul Stappert" written on it. His hands shook when he opened the folder.

Henkie looked over his shoulder.

"Got something?"

DeKok took a deep breath.

"Graph paper."

"How was Manneke Pis?"

Vledder shook his head.

"You should get more familiar with our southern

neighbors," he said. "Manneke Pis is in Brussels. I was in Antwerp."

DeKok spread his arms wide.

"I thought you would have taken the opportunity to visit Brussels to have a look at the famous statue."

DeKok was referring to the statue of a urinating urchin, the symbol of Brussels. Although the statue is nude, the city has provided hundreds of different uniforms and outfits for the little boy. The statue is dressed appropriately for certain festivals and celebrations and on some days the statue will "urinate" wine for all comers.

"As you know," said Vledder, "I did get a travel voucher for Antwerp only. No side trips allowed. Aren't you the one always reminds me about the lack of deep pockets in the police department? I know I'm not paying for diversion."

DeKok laughed. He knew full well that Dutch police personnel abroad often had to dig in their own pockets, or had to rely on the hospitality of the foreign colleagues, to avoid hunger and thirst.

"So, tell me about Long Jack."

"He's not feeling too good. He's looking at many years of hard time. We surround every criminal with love and concern by comparison to Belgium. They don't think like the Dutch. Belgian officials look at their primary function as punishment, not rehabilitation."

"But what did he say?"

Vledder grinned.

"His first instinct was to clam up. Steven Visser, the narcotics guy, tried, but Long Jack wasn't talking. Narcotics wanted Santen to roll over. They hoped to bust a complete distribution line."

"But he wasn't selling out?"

"Well he wasn't about to be used. Steven tried to lure him, you know. He was pretending to know more than he knew. He speculated aloud the trail might very well end in Laren. But Long Jack didn't bite."

"Did you have the feeling that he knew what Visser was talking about?"

"For sure. He smirked, but refused to give a verbal response. He didn't even give up his contact on the ship. The Belgian police are interrogating the whole crew, but it's shooting fish in a barrel. Santen's contact will probably sail in a few days, with no one the wiser." He paused and consulted his computer screen. Vledder always transcribed his notes to the computer as soon as possible. "Yes," he continued, "Visser kept insisting and then Santen finally lost his cool, in a way. He told Visser he should be glad to have confiscated the drugs and to quit nagging him. 'As long as farmers starve and poppies flower,' he said, 'you have a job.' And then he started to stare at the ceiling, ignoring Visser completely."

"Did Steven get angry?"

Vledder shook his head.

"I don't think the guy has a temper. Once he realized Santen wasn't playing, he walked away from the inter-rogation. As he left, he shook hands with Long Jack, like one diplomat to another. He actually thanked him for his cooperation and said he looked forward to seeing him again, soon. Long Jack played the part well. He bowed and said that it had been his pleasure."

DeKok smiled. He knew the laconic Visser well. Before he had transferred to narcotics, Visser had worked with DeKok at Warmoes Street Station for a number of years.

"How did you do? Did you get anything?"

Vledder shook his head and touched a few keys on his keyboard.

"The pickings were slim. To start I got about as far as Steven. He kept his mouth shut, except to admit knowing Jan Rouwen ... a boy he sometimes met in Utrecht. According to him that was it. He admitted to lending Rouwen his apartment for a few days. Said it was only to give the boy an opportunity to meet a woman. His mother apparently objected to the girl and would not let her in the house. Rouwen had to take her somewhere, didn't he?"

"How sweet."

Vledder ignored that.

"Santen's shell started to crack, when I told him we lifted his prints from Erik Bavel's room. He must have realized there was no way he could deny having been there. Of course, I asked him what they had been looking for."

"Aha ... and?"

"He looked at me for a long time ... like he wanted to tell me. Then he said he couldn't—he'd promised someone he would not tell."

"Did he at least tell you whom he had promised?"

"No, he didn't want to tell me that, either. So I asked him whether he searched the rooms on his own initiative, or on orders from someone."

"And it was on orders from someone."

"Yes, but he refused to identify the principal. Then I thought about your feeling Santen had been the victim of Haarveld's betrayal."

"And you pursued it?"

"Yes."

"Any good?"

"He looked shocked. He thought for a while. Then he made a proposal."

"What kind of proposal?"

"If we were able to make a deal with the prosecutor in Belgium that would allow him to do his time in Holland, rather than Belgium, he would—"

"Yes, yes, yes," interrupted DeKok impatiently.

"He would deliver the killer of Jean-Paul Stappert and Erik Bavel."

17

DeKok was restless again. Reports were piling up on his desk waiting for him to sign off so Vledder could submit them to the commissaris. Sitting untouched was a report to the judge-advocate he was to have approved over a month before. Little of the information on his desk had anything to do with the current case. The bulk of the cases were already closed for all practical purposes. As usual, DeKok was late with the paperwork. His only consolation was in knowing Vledder had already filed all the preliminary reports. Vledder was as trusty as his computer. In some cases he had only to record the verdict to close the file.

DeKok wasn't meant to be a bureaucrat, to him it was pointless concentrating on stale material. He was singularly focused on the current case, now more than a month old.

He could not remember a case lasting this long. Murders were supposed to be solved rapidly. In Holland they were. There simply were not many murders, compared to other countries. The homicide detail for the entire city of Amsterdam was smaller than that in a single New York police station. Homicide detectives were spread out. He and Vledder were the only homicide detectives in Warmoes Street Station. Other one- and two-person teams were spread out over half the remaining station houses in the city. There was also a relatively large detail at headquarters—individual teams could call on the group at headquarters for support. The rest, such as CSI, pathology, and the crime lab had to be shared with all the branches, from narcotics to the traffic police.

Therefore, individual cases fell heavily on the small homicide squads in stations where they were assigned. Most seasoned officers considered it a haphazard system. DeKok reflected how well it had worked until now. Until the present, he and his colleagues at Warmoes Street had handled a relatively light caseload.

But these "boardinghouse murders," as the newspapers called them, were an enigma. They could end up in the cold case files, simply, for lack of evidence. A month had passed and all he had was vague conjecture. There was no clear motive—nothing pointed to a specific suspect. He had no sense of direction.

Even if he regained his sense of direction, how would he get enough evidence for an arrest, let alone, legal grounds for a conviction?

With a grunt of disgust he swept the paper work in a drawer and stood up. He started to pace up and down the large detective room.

He had to go back all the way to the night in question, now more than a month ago. He remembered how his mind seemed to be pushed in different directions at that time. He'd put aside the unsettling sense someone had tried to telepathically communicate with him. He was certain of one thing—he'd had a temporary window into the soul of the strangler.

He stopped in front of the window and rocked slightly up and down on the balls of his feet. Across the street he looked into the alley where Moshe, the herring man, kept his cart. The alley was empty, but in his mind's eye he could see Moshe clearly. How often, he thought, have I stood here? It was generally when a crime had been insoluble at first sight. Somehow the view of the rooftops and the narrow, smelly streets never failed to inspire him. He needed one of those brilliant insights now.

He could never convince his colleagues he'd experienced some psychic phenomenon the night the boys were found strangled. Dick Vledder would laugh at him—who wouldn't. He was certain Jean-Paul Stappert had communicated a kind of distress signal. When Alex Waardenburg hinted at the same experience, he validated DeKok's recollection.

No judge-advocate would act on his gut instinct. He needed solid motive, opportunity, and, at the very least, circumstantial evidence. Anything less would result in a defense attorney humiliating him at the opening and shredding the case. He hadn't even enough to detain a suspect for interrogation.

He pushed his chin out and lifted his head. By force of will he put those ideas aside. He would have to keep both feet firmly planted on the ground and re-examine the facts. It was his only hope—he still had a window of opportunity. He'd make it suffice.

The phone on his desk rang. Vledder reached over to pick it up. After a few seconds he replaced the receiver, stood up, and tapped DeKok on the shoulder.

"Commissaris Buitendam wants to talk to you." He raised a finger in the air and smiled. "Be nice to the man. He cannot take too many shocks. He is recovering from the flu."

The commissaris was pale. His skin seemed even more transparent and his eyes were dull. The flu had hit him hard.

DeKok noticed it and, much to his own surprise, felt a wave of pity for his boss.

Buitendam waved toward a heavy-set man in one of the chairs.

"I don't have to introduce Mr. Van Mechelen to you."

DeKok shook his head.

"It has been a mixed pleasure," he said blandly, "to have met the learned counsel on a few occasions."

The commissaris was probably still too ill to react. He ignored the remark.

"Mr. Van Mechelen," said Buitendam tiredly, "has made contact with his client, Ramon Bavel, or vice versa. The young man has acquainted his family with his whereabouts."

"What a relief," interrupted DeKok.

Buitendam closed his eyes and then opened them again.

"Indeed," he agreed. "His family is quite relieved. Ramon would like to return home and hearth, but he still fears an arrest. After consulting with the judge-advocate, attorney Van Mechelen asks us to guarantee Ramon Bavel will not be arrested upon his return to the Netherlands ... not in connection with the boardinghouse murders."

"So, Ramon is abroad?"

The lawyer slowly rose from his chair. He apparently had some trouble moving his bulk.

"Of course I cannot confirm his exact whereabouts," he said slowly, gathering his breath. "Attorney-client privilege prevents me from revealing our conversation. Early on we assumed your investigation would be rapidly concluded. You have a certain reputation in these matters," he added with grudging admiration in his voice. "That is why I advised Ramon to stay away for a time. The idea was for him to return as soon as the air cleared, you understand? We hoped by now you'd have the real murderer in custody."

DeKok smiled.

"And now that results have eluded us and the investigation continues, Ramon is getting impatient."

"Exactly," nodded the lawyer. "You must know it is very frustrating to be innocent and still be banished."

DeKok gave the lawyer a penetrating look.

"He imposed the banishment upon himself. Nobody forced him. But," he added slowly, "you might consider the possible connection between the poor results of the ongoing investigation and the fact that Ramon is out of my reach."

Van Mechelen started to get agitated.

"Ramon is innocent," he exclaimed.

"How do you know?"

"He told me so."

"And you took his declaration of innocence at face value?"

The over-sized attorney calmed down a little. He sighed.

"Ramon tells me the truth. Aside from my fiduciary responsibility, our relationship is based on mutual trust."

DeKok rubbed a little finger on the bridge of his nose. It was one of his characteristic gestures when he felt in control of a situation.

"I always had a very good relationship with my mother. It was a relationship based on mutual trust *and* love. Yet I lied to her a number of times in my younger years ... simply because I felt she didn't need to know everything."

The lawyer shook his head.

"That ... that ... eh," he protested, "is something else altogether. The relationship between a client and a defense attorney must be completely open—he knows I cannot function as his legal counsel otherwise."

DeKok nodded agreement.

"I understand your position completely," he said soothingly. "You say Ramon swears he knows nothing. You believe him innocent of the boardinghouse murders. I understand that you take that position as your own. After all, you have never had a client who lied to you."

Van Mechelen bridled.

"It is not a position ... it's the truth."

DeKok again made a soothing gesture.

"A truth," he repeated. "A truth in which you believe."

"Without reservation."

"In that case I know you will not object to my interrogating Ramon in your presence. I'll even allow you to determine the place ... in the Netherlands."

Van Mechelen knew DeKok had him by the short hairs. His round, gleaming face was devoid of expression. Long minutes passed in silence, then he pointed at DeKok.

"You'll hear from me."

Without ceremony, he turned on his heels and left.

Commissaris Buitendam came from behind his desk and looked at DeKok with a hint of admiration in his eyes.

"You did well, DeKok. I think I should tell you that."

The old sleuth smiled. He looked at the pale face. There was a sheen of perspiration on the forehead.

"You best get better, soon," he advised kindly.

Vledder was interested when his colleague returned to the detective room.

"And, were you decent to the commissaris?"

"Very, I even wished him good health."

"You're making progress," laughed Vledder.

DeKok nodded sagely.

"He is, too," he said.

"Did you discuss Santen's proposal?"

"Not yet. I'll keep it up my sleeve as a last resort. Personally, I'd rather not. That kind of bargain takes up a lot of time. We'd have to convince both the Belgian and the Dutch authorities. Once we do we have no way of knowing whether Santen can deliver." He grinned ruefully. "It is investing in the word of a criminal trying to deal his way out of hard time."

"You don't think he knows the murderer?"

"Given his connections and background, he probably knows something. It wouldn't surprise me if he were involved with the murders. The question is are we buying what he's selling. I won't be manipulated, especially not by a character like Long Jack." He looked into the distance for a while. "You know," he went on, "I've seen smart, seasoned cops go nuts chasing fictitious people, places, and events. These jokers count on us to be conscientious. I'll bet you Santen is as opportunistic as a vulture. We'd be making a bargain with the Devil, if we delay our investigation to sweeten his 'deal.' It isn't happening on my watch. We could never reverse any deal we make with the Belgians. We cannot propose to take him into custody here and reserve the right to give him back, if things don't work out."

Vledder looked abashed.

"He sounded so convincing," said the younger man. "He appeared to know what he was talking about and he meant what he said."

DeKok smiled an encouraging smile.

"You could be quite right. Just know the pitfalls of this sort of proposal. It can be a quagmire for police officers who are sincerely interested in clearing their cases." He smiled again. "Anyway," he continued cheerfully, "I've made a proposal of my own."

"To whom?"

"To Mr. Gerard Van Mechelen, Esquire, himself."

"Oh, was he in the office with the boss?"

"He wanted a guarantee we would not arrest Ramon for the murders … should he happen to return home."

"You didn't give him a guarantee!"

DeKok shook his head.

"No, I said that I wanted to interrogate Ramon in the presence of his lawyer in a place of his choosing."

"And the fat cat lawyer agreed?"

DeKok looked at the clock on the wall.

"He'll be in earnest conversation with his client at this time."

"If they agree, and Ramon comes back to Holland, will you arrest him?"

Neither DeKok nor Vledder heard the knock on the door, but both saw the shape of a large figure against the frosted glass of the door. They watched as one of the detectives yelled for the visitor to enter. The door opened slowly to reveal the figure of Alex Waardenburg. He approached DeKok's desk with a vague smile on his face.

DeKok met him halfway.

"Mr. Waardenburg," said DeKok heartily. "What a

surprise." He led the visitor to his desk and pulled out a chair. "Please, have a seat."

With a theatrical gesture, Waardenburg swept his cape over one shoulder and took a seat.

"Curiosity compelled me to come," said the musician. "I have not read anything further in the newspapers. Do you have the perpetrator in your sights?"

DeKok shook his head, a sad look on his face.

"The investigation is not progressing as I had hoped," he admitted. "But we're by no means defeated."

"Do you have an inkling ... a prime suspect?"

DeKok again shook his head, this time with a wan smile.

"Hardly. In fact I'm at a dead end unlike any in my career, especially considering the amount of time we have worked on this."

Alex Waardenburg stared at the inspector for a moment with a sympathetic, but searching expression on his face.

"You look tired." It sounded concerned. "You need some amusement, some relaxation." He felt in an inner pocket. "I want to invite you and your colleague to a concert." He handed over two tickets. "My son, Kiliaan, will be performing some of his own piano compositions, accompanied by the Municipal Symphony Orchestra."

"Where?"

"Here in Amsterdam, of course. In the Concert Gebouw, one of the few concert halls with perfect acoustics. Kiliaan received a number of offers through our impresario. We rejected them—they were for smaller venues. Only after the Concert Gebouw became available, did we accept. We're thrilled to have the opportunity."

DeKok did not react at once. He studied the round, fleshy face, the red, veined cheeks, the dark moustache."

"Who," he asked softly, "is your impresario?"

Waardenburg seemed to be surprised by the question, but he answered readily.

"He's actually my son's impresario, of course. I'm a member of the orchestra. But it is Haarveld … Willy Haarveld."

18

Vledder shook his head as he looked at the two tickets Waardenburg had left behind.

"The longer I live the less I understand about people," he sighed. "Alex Waardenburg and his son know Willy Haarveld has a sleazy reputation. The man is a swindler ... and, yet, he's representing them as their agent." He paused, studied the tickets. "Did you know anything about a connection between Haarveld and the Waardenburgs?"

"No."

Vledder shivered visibly.

"Everybody knows everybody and everything seems to mesh. It's a small, suffocating mud puddle in which we have landed." He looked directly at DeKok. "You think maybe that the Waardenburgs are part of Haarveld's distribution system?"

"Not the drugs again."

"Sure," said Vledder. "Why not? Waardenburg has a bunch of rich kids whose mommies and daddies pay him to develop their talent—they'd be like low-hanging fruit for a dealer."

DeKok picked up the tickets and studied them.

"Not much time," he said pensively. "It's scheduled for next week."

"The concert?"

"Yes."

"And do you plan to go?"

DeKok pulled on his lower lip and let it plop back. He did that several times. Vledder became restless.

"Come on," urged the young man.

"Alex Waardenburg," said DeKok slowly, "wasn't all that curious. He's perfectly aware we're stuck. He may not know what we have, but he knows it isn't enough" DeKok tapped the tickets with his fingers. "He isn't all that generous, either, giving two tireless public servants a chance for much-needed recreation. He has his own agenda."

"Probably, but what is it?"

Before DeKok could answer, Commissaris Buitendam entered the detective room. His appearance caused all conversation to stop. All eyes followed him as he made his way to DeKok's desk. DeKok stood up as the commissaris approached. Buitendam threw a note on DeKok's desk.

"I just got off the telephone with Mr. Van Mechelen. He agrees to your proposal. You may interrogate Ramon Bavel. His attorney expects you at that address—three o'clock sharp."

DeKok picked up the note.

"Winterswijk," he read out loud. "That's practically on the German border.

Commissaris Buitendam nodded.

"Mr. Van Mechelen has everything arranged. At three o'clock Ramon will also be in that neighborhood." He pointed at the note. "That's not the place for the interrogation. You will only meet the lawyer there. He will lead you the rest of the way." The commissaris gave DeKok a long look. "Therefore it will not be necessary to alert the local police."

DeKok grimaced.

"That Van Mechelen ... he thinks of everything."

Because one of the lawyer's conditions had been for DeKok to go alone, he went by train. He took the InterCity to Apeldoorn, transferring to a local connector that eventually deposited him in Winterswijk.

He asked the way to the modern Town Hall and in front of the monument to those fallen in WWII he found Mr. Van Mechelen. DeKok approached and shook hands.

"Where's Ramon?"

The lawyer smiled.

"You'll have to be patient a little longer."

Carefully checking whether or not they were being tailed, the lawyer led DeKok to a small side street. A long, black, chauffeured limousine was waiting. Van Mechelen directed DeKok to the back seat. The heavy-set lawyer followed and the car immediately started moving.

Suddenly DeKok discovered that the windows in the back of the limo were blacked out. He gave the lawyer a mocking look.

"Isn't this a bit melodramatic? It's like an old-fashioned *ride* you read about in gangster novels. Or is this a kidnapping?"

Van Mechelen shook his head.

"Everything I do," he said pedantically, "is for the protection of my client. I will bring you in a round-a-bout way to an open place in the woods. You'll never know whether you're in Holland, or in Germany." There was a self-satisfied grin on his face. "You see," he continued smugly, "you'll never be sure, as required by law, whether you are bound by the protocols prescribed for interrogation by Holland or by Germany. You have no search warrant in Germany, nor can you make an arrest in that country."

"We agreed I would meet Ramon on Dutch soil."

"You'll have to guess whether I'm keeping my word."

DeKok gazed at the conceited expression on the lawyer's face and decided to let it rest. He nodded to himself and remained silent for the rest of the trip.

After about half an hour the car stopped. Van Mechelen asked DeKok to get out. They found themselves on a wide sand path, surrounded by old forest. DeKok looked for any signs of his exact whereabouts, but found none.

The corpulent lawyer puffed toward a side road, no more than a narrow footpath. They reached an open spot in the woods. It was a picnic area. A few tables were scattered about and a large trashcan was chained to a post in the center. A young man was seated at one of the tables. As DeKok approached he recognized a similarity between the young man's face and that of the elder Bavel.

The young man rose and gave a formal bow.

"Inspector DeKok," he greeted.

"With a kay-oh-kay," reacted DeKok almost automatically. "I made a long, clandestine, journey to meet you," he added calmly.

The young man smiled.

"The arrangements are those of Mr. Van Mechelen. He's always very discreet."

They took a seat at the table across from each other. DeKok studied Ramon's face. He looked exactly like his father, just younger and dressed in running attire. Ramon nervously fumbled with his jacket zipper.

"I'm innocent."

He sounded passionate.

"Then, why did you run away?"

Ramon hesitated.

"You won't like the answer," he replied. "Frankly I have little faith in the Dutch justice system and even less faith in the law, as it is practiced in Amsterdam. I've studied law for a few years and I know what I'm talking about." He paused, looking for the right words. "Long ago we had class justice. Notable or wealthy people were handled in a different, milder way. The full weight of the law would only be applied to the poor, people who were powerless in the society. Not any more. Now we have what people like you call classless justice, but with an important difference. Sociopaths—criminals, drug addicts—have nothing to fear from Lady Justitia. In that scenario I could rely on her compassion, even mildness." For the first time he looked DeKok full in the face. "But," he went on, "I'm no sociopath. I have no criminal record ... I'm not substance addicted. Oh, but I have one severe handicap, a wealthy, prominent father. The full weight of the law will fall on me at the slightest provocation. The media will pick up on even the smallest misdemeanor. That's why I fled when Kiliaan Waardenburg told me that you suspect me."

DeKok made a resigned gesture. He had heard the argument before—it was so tiresome. It was not true, but he was not here to debate Ramon Bavel's skewed opinion of Dutch jurisprudence.

"You're entitled to your opinion of the law," he said. "Just one thing—how would a poor youth manage to withdraw in luxurious exile? Where would he find an anxious parent with deep pockets? How would he come by a well-heeled lawyer, complete with chauffeured limousine?"

Ramon shrugged his shoulders.

"I told you that you wouldn't like my answer ... but it *is* the motivation behind my flight, as an innocent person." He paused and then gave DeKok a pensive look. "You can't really suspect me of the stranglings?"

DeKok looked at the trees and listened to the birds. He looked back at Ramon. There was intelligence there, he thought, warped intelligence, maybe. But Ramon obviously possessed a strong character.

"Your behavior after the deaths of your brothers, Erik and Ricky, didn't reveal much sensitivity."

Ramon smiled sadly.

"That depends on who you ask. You've obviously been influenced by their mother."

"Their mother?"

DeKok was annoyed. He had not taken that into account.

"Sure. My own mother died before I was two. She died in a traffic accident. Father re-married—Erik and Ricky are my half-brothers. Whatever you heard from my stepmother the boys started taking drugs, all on their own. Both became addicts, all on their own. When I confronted them for their lack of will power, they challenged me to a test. For a while I would use the same amount of drugs as they did. It was childish and dangerous, but it would prove me strong enough to take the heroin or leave it. They were furious because I passed the test with flying colors. Whether out of revenge or to manipulate their mother, Erik and Ricky turned it around. Suddenly I was the one who challenged *them* to a test, getting them addicted. It was a filthy lie, but their mother believed it and perpetuated it. The so-called party after Ricky's death is just one more fairy tale."

DeKok was at a loss.

"But why?" he demanded.

Ramon sighed.

"There was no love lost—what child wouldn't resist accepting a new mother. She saw me as a threat to her and her relationship with my father. The woman has her own demons. She blamed herself for Ricky's death ... and with reason."

"How is that?"

The young man nervously bit his lower lip and gave his lawyer a helpless look. The lawyer was seated at the same table but had not entered the conversation. Now he spoke for the first time.

"Mrs. Bavel," said Van Mechelen brusquely, "is a long time addict. She supplied Erik and Ricky early in their drug use."

DeKok rubbed his face with a flat hand. Then he shook his head.

"She was an addict herself?"

The lawyer nodded gravely.

"It was the reason Mr. Bavel distanced himself from her and her sons."

DeKok returned to the young man.

"Where did she get her drugs?"

"I don't know exactly ... Laren, I think."

When DeKok returned late in the evening to the Warmoes Street Station, he was surprised to find Vledder still working. The young inspector was busy on his computer. Vledder pushed the keyboard away. With a smile he looked at his old partner.

"I knew you'd stop by here before going home. How did it go? Did you arrest Ramon?"

DeKok shook his weary head.

"Mr. Van Mechelen played a nice little trick on me."

"On you?"

"Yes," DeKok told Vledder how he had been tricked.

"So," concluded Vledder, "although the agreement was to have the meeting in Holland, you could not be sure?"

"That's right. I could not know if I was on firm legal ground, or not. Van Mechelen made sure I knew that as well. So, there was no way for me to possibly exceed my authority in front of three witnesses."

"Three witnesses?"

"Ramon Bavel, his lawyer, and the driver."

Vledder shook his head in commiseration.

"What a rip off."

DeKok grinned.

"On the way back he told me that he had kept his word and that we had never left Dutch soil."

Vledder snorted.

"But by then Ramon was out of reach again."

"Exactly."

"So, what are we going to do about Ramon?"

DeKok did not answer at once. He recalled the picture of the young man in the woods.

"Ramon Bavel is an intelligent young man. He and Van Mechelen are a formidable team. If we hope to achieve anything at all, we must have clear, irrefutable, evidence. And as long as we don't have that ..." He did not finish the sentence, but sat down behind his desk and opened a drawer. He took out the tickets they had received from Alex Waardenburg and tossed them over to Vledder.

"I want another thirteen tickets like that," he said.
"Another thirteen ... what for?"
DeKok gave him a friendly grin.
"For a cultural club ... music lovers."

19

A feeling of extreme tension came over DeKok. It slithered surreptitiously to his throat and threatened to close it. Next he felt it in the extremities, tingling like a light electrical charge. He knew he was taking unacceptable risks. If his plan failed, it would have far-reaching consequences for himself, as well as the entire Amsterdam Municipal Police Force. He could almost see the headlines and could hear the angry questions in the Senate.

If he wanted to solve the boardinghouse murders, it *had* to happen now ... and in the manner that he had planned.

It was an all or nothing gamble. The prize was a triple murderer. DeKok's hope was concentrated on a psychological bomb and the clock was ticking. When he revealed the unimaginable truth, he counted on the perpetrator to betray himself. Surprise was on his side.

He looked at young Vledder. Vledder guessed his strategy, and looked worried behind his desk. The young man was well aware of the risks. DeKok's attention turned to the two inspectors he had borrowed from another station house. Joop Klaver and Jan Kuiper always worked as a team. They had readily agreed to help Vledder and DeKok.

With a nervous gesture he pushed up the sleeve of his jacket and looked at his watch, comparing it to the clock on the wall. They should be just about here, the members of his culture club—a somewhat mocking name for a segment of Little Lowee's clientele.

He sighed a deep sigh of relief when at the agreed upon time, a knock on the door announced the arrival of Little Lowee. Within the next ten minutes all had arrived. Little Lowee wore a dark suit with a subdued tie. Everyone looked to be in their Sunday best. A few even wore evening clothes.

Inspector Kuiper sidled up to DeKok. He had recognized most of the visitors.

"What do you want with these Baker Street Irregulars?" he asked in a whisper. "I count four pimps, three retired whores, a call girl, a barkeeper, a fence, and a card shark."

DeKok smiled but did not answer.

He pulled chairs together and invited them to be seated. Then he bade them welcome and explained their role.

Once DeKok had answered their questions, everyone went downstairs and waited in the lobby of the station house for the taxis. The cabs arrived at the appointed time and the convoy drove off toward the Concert Gebouw.

They alighted from the cars in front of the main entrance. A bit uneasily they took their seats on the last row to either side of the center aisle. Klaver and Kuiper took their positions elsewhere. Their assignments were different.

The members of the Municipal Symphonic Orchestra were already seated on the stage. The concertmaster made a gesture and the oboe blew a clear A. The other musicians tuned their instruments accordingly and for a short time the hall was filled with the individual sounds and some tone ladders of the various instruments as the musicians tested their adjustments.

Red Lena leaned closer to DeKok. The overpowering fragrance of her perfume almost choked him.

"Have they started yet?" she whispered hoarsely.

DeKok shook his head. He realized that some of his guests had never before attended a live concert.

DeKok stretched himself and looked at the stage. In the foreground, the leader of the second violins, Alex Waardenburg, sat placidly with his violin resting on one knee. He leaned forward and carefully adjusted the placement of his music stand. With his bow he flipped a few pages of the music and then flipped them back. It was a quick and practiced gesture that showed great expertise.

The grey sleuth let his eyes wander. The large auditorium was almost completely filled. There were few empty seats. Even the seats on the stage, behind the orchestra were nearly all filled.

On the first row, directly behind the orchestra he discovered Willy Haarveld in a shiny purple sharkskin suit. It was reassuring. Although he had been assured the impresario would attend the performance, it was a relief to notice his presence on the stage.

On stage left, at the grand piano, was the soloist for the evening, Kiliaan Waardenburg. The young man was in tails and looked immaculate. He was obviously tense. His blond hair glistened in the stage lights.

The audience waited for the conductor.

One more time DeKok checked on the members of his culture club. Kuiper's appellation of them as the Baker Street Irregulars was humorous, but not exactly correct. They looked the part. Only someone who knew their true identity would have found anything odd about the gathering. DeKok smiled to himself. He loved the group who, although living on the edge of society themselves, had immediately agreed to help him this evening in his fight against crime.

He frowned. Perhaps that was a bit too idealistic. Little Lowee wouldn't be above a little larceny—he could have blackmailed them into cooperating. The diminutive barkeeper wasn't above street tactics.

He rubbed the bridge of his nose. In reality he couldn't care less as to how Lowee had achieved his goals. They were here, that's what counted. He hoped with all his heart they would be able to act when the time came.

DeKok glanced aside at Vledder, who was seated next to Little Lowee. The young inspector was perceptibly nervous. Now that the time was near, the entire group showed some signs of nervousness. Even Red Lena, whose sharp tongue was feared by the most reckless criminals in the Quarter, plucked nervously at the buttons of her blouse.

The house lights dimmed, and the conductor descended the staircase. The audience applauded. The members of the orchestra rose. The orchestra sat down as soon as the conductor reached his position behind the podium. The conductor waited for the applause to die down. He tapped his baton on the side of the lectern and the performance commenced.

The audience listened to the first half of the performance in respectful silence. The piano was used as part of the rhythm section. But after the intermission, when Kiliaan Waardenburg became the soloist, DeKok's little group started to stir. Little Lowee nodded vehemently. The others made various motions of agreement as well. When Kiliaan repeated a theme, Red Lena suddenly stood up. The others followed suit.

DeKok realized he had to take control of the situation immediately. He signaled Vledder. They both left their seats and stood in the aisle. The culture club noisily bunched up behind the two inspectors.

At a slow, but deliberate pace they advanced toward the stage. The group became noisier and some balled fists were waved in the air. The audience noticed the disturbance and became restless. Some of them stood up to better see the commotion in the aisle.

The conductor saw the unrest among his orchestra and suddenly waved his baton in a cutting gesture. The music ebbed away. The noise in the hall increased.

Ever more threatening, the group came closer and Red Lena yelled: *"Murderer"* The cry was picked up and repeated by the rest of the group. Vledder and DeKok increased their speed and each walked toward one of the stairs at either side that led to the stage.

There was pandemonium among the orchestra. This was unthinkable—it wasn't a rock concert. This was a sacrosanct symphonic performance. Music stands fell to the floor. In disarray the musicians scattered and stumbled as they tried to safeguard their instruments.

Later DeKok would remember what happened after that as a movie in slow motion. He saw the large figure of Alex Waardenburg come at him. His round, fleshy face was pale with rage. His eyes had a murderous gleam.

Out of the corner of his eyes he saw Kiliaan sprint up the stairs in back of the stage ... straight into the arms of Inspector Klaver. Alex Waardenburg raised his violin into the air. DeKok saw it coming, but he was momentarily transfixed. The instrument smashed his head. Just before he hit the floor he saw Willy Haarveld, who stood like a purple statue at the back of the stage.

Then everything turned black.

Mrs. DeKok opened the door.

Dick Vledder stood in the front doorway, flanked by Klaver and Kuiper. Vledder carried a heavy fruit basket.

"We came to visit the patient," he grinned, "Do old sleuths get visiting hours?"

Mrs. DeKok laughed.

"You better not let him hear that. He doesn't feel ill at all. He's just angry to have allowed that pansy to hit him with a fiddle. The doctor wants him to rest for at least two weeks, never mind keeping him housebound. He was in the House of Keeping yesterday, interviewing people."

The *Huis van Bewaring,* literally the "House of Keeping" is the place where suspects are kept before sentencing. It is like a very liberal jail. People are locked up in regular, though spartan, rooms, not cells. They can order meals sent in and have daily access to visitors. They were treated as suspects, not convicts.

Vledder nodded.

"Doesn't surprise me," he said. "I know him."

The inspectors entered the living room.

DeKok waved cordially from a large easy chair next to the fireplace. On a small table next to him stood a bottle of fine cognac and a number of large snifters. A telephone call from the station house had forewarned him of the visit. He had taken the necessary steps and uncorked a bottle.

Vledder placed he fruit basket at his feet.

"This is from the colleagues. Everyone wishes you a speedy recovery."

DeKok waved a hand in the air.

"Take it away. That's for a sick person. And I'm not

.sick." It sounded obstreperous.

Vledder shook his head and looked around for a chair to sit on.

"Can't get our money back. You're stuck with it," he said, as he sat down.

DeKok smiled resignedly while he waved the others to chairs.

"All right. Leave it there. I know an old person somewhere who'd be happy to get it. Sit down and I'll pour."

With a rich sound the golden liquid filled the glasses. DeKok was a connoisseur of good cognac, a passion he shared with Little Lowee.

Kuiper leaned forward to receive his glass.

"Don't mind if I do," he said, "but that's not why we came. You asked us to help, dragged us to the Concert Gebouw, and caused a big noise. Joop and I want to know what this is all about." He pointed at Vledder. "That one has told us a few things, but we don't really understand all the sound and fury."

DeKok made sure every one had a glass. Then he raised his own glass.

"Proost," he said, "here's to crime."

Mrs. DeKok came in and placed two large platters of delicacies on the sideboard.

"You're always telling me, Jurriaan," she chided, "that you should never salute crime ... you should toast *against* it."

"You're right," answered her husband. "Here's *against* crime." And he raised his glass for the second time and then took a sip.

He fell back in his easy chair. He gently rocked the glass in his hand and sniffed the aroma. Then he took another, larger sip and placed the glass on the table next to him.

"This has been," he began, "the most difficult, frustrating, and weirdest murder case of my career. The main problem was motive. Two young men, recovered addicts, are strangled. Soon to follow is their landlady. She's a much older woman and, from all accounts, not always so nurturing. There was no common thread between these victims outside of a rather tenuous business relationship. Erik and Jean-Paul were friends, maybe even, confidants—did they have some sort of partnership? In combination with the housekeeper? Or was there an individual motive for each killing? Whatever I tried, nothing fit."

"You're talking about the boardinghouse murders," confirmed Klaver.

"Yes. From the very get go my own perceptions led me astray. Jean-Paul Stappert was musically gifted ... maybe a genius, with a head full of melodies. But Jean-Paul Stappert could not write music, not a single note. The melodies were in his head. That's all he had. To kill Jean-Paul to steal his compositions would be senseless, hardly a motive for murder. When he died his music would die with him."

"That seems very reasonable," observed Kuiper. "I don't see how your thinking was off."

"It took a long time before I discovered how wrong I was. During a covert search, with an un-named accomplice, I discovered a folder with the title 'Jean-Paul Stappert' on it. I found it in Laren ... in the desk of Willy Haarveld. The folder was filled with two sheets of graph paper."

"Graph paper?" asked Klaver. "What sort of graph paper?"

DeKok sighed.

"Large sheets with tiny blue-lined squares on it. Vledder and I had found a pad of the identical paper in Erik

Bavel's room. We took it to the lab, but they could only tell us there were some vague impressions of small lines and dots on the top sheets.", stated Klaver. "No wonder you said nothing. You didn't have a search warrant, did you?"

"No," admitted DeKok, "and I would prefer if you forgot all about that."

"No problem, go on."

"It puzzled me why Willy Haarveld kept two sheets of graph paper, filled with little lines and dots. There had to be a meaning behind the seemingly random markings. I also knew through Little Lowee, Jean-Paul had been in contact with the impresario to discuss his melodies," DeKok took another sip. As strange as it seems it wasn't until days later I realized the hen scratches on the graph paper were music."

"You never told me that," said Vledder.

"Sorry, I thought I had," said DeKok without remorse, knowing full well he had neglected to tell Vledder because the notion had seemed too outrageous to him at the time.

Vledder raised his eyebrows; he was well aware of DeKok's almost infallible memory.

"Anyway," resumed DeKok, "Jean-Paul had actually put those melodies of his down on paper. Since he could not read or write music, he developed a system of his own. He used graph paper, because it was the easiest way to make his notations of dots and little lines. The only limitation was he, alone, could read the music. Without considerable instruction, nobody else would be able to discern his system."

DeKok paused to take another sip of cognac. Mrs. DeKok handed one of the platters to Vledder, who helped himself to some of the food. Then he passed the platter on to Kuiper. Klaver urged DeKok on.

"Very well," DeKok resumed his narrative. "After

meeting with Willy Haarveld, Jean-Paul knew the self-styled impresario was incapable of deciphering the code. He decided to learn composition, so he could transcribe his melodies in regular music script and thus—"

"He wound up with Alex Waardenburg," interrupted Vledder.

"Exactly," agreed DeKok. "Waardenburg was a rich music teacher with only rich students. Whatever his flaws Waardenburg recognized at once he had found a musical genius in Jean-Paul. Let me point out that Alex never intended to kill Jean-Paul. He just wanted the music, the melodies. From the start he raved about the melodies—said they were harmonically perfect and contained refined transpositions. He talked of another Mozart. I was led astray because he was self-satisfied, not to say self-impressed. His ambition was for his son. Not satisfied with his son's desire to become a concert pianist, he dreamed of making his Kiliaan into a world-renowned composer, as well as a concert pianist."

DeKok paused. He silently reviewed the case. The plot of the drama was clear in his head. He couldn't get over his amazement for taking so long to unravel it.

"Jean-Paul was on fire," he went on, "he was thrilled to talk about his melodies, to explain his code. Naively he told Waardenburg there were drawers full of his compositions in Erik's room."

Vledder snorted.

"He was begging to be killed."

"Perhaps. But it took an incident … a spark to inflame the tragic proceedings. Jean-Paul told Kiliaan he had contacted Haarveld a second time. This time he'd left a few sheets of manuscripts, those ones on the graph paper."

"And you found those," concluded Klaver.

"Kiliaan was enraged. He did not want anyone else to see the sheets. He wrote a threatening letter to Haarveld, warning him to keep his hands off Jean-Paul's music. He also tried to get Jean-Paul to change his mind—urged him to get the sheets back and break off all contact with Haarveld. At home, in the presence of his domineering, ambitious father, Kiliaan dared not broach the subject. Jean-Paul went to the house on the night of the murder. Kiliaan was waiting for him. On the edge of the canal, between the parked cars, they quarreled. When Jean-Paul refused to retrieve the sheets and sever his relationship with Haarveld, Kiliaan snapped. He gripped Jean-Paul by the throat and strangled him."

"And nobody saw it?" asked Kuiper.

DeKok shook his head.

"It's a quiet canal. Most of the houses have been converted to offices. There's almost no one around after dark. Of course, we asked around, but nobody saw anything."

"Come on," urged Vledder, "what else did Kiliaan do?"

"Well, I heard most of this only yesterday, you understand. But according to him, Kiliaan walked around in a daze afterwards. Then he realized what he had done and weighed his chances. That's when he remembered the wealth of music in Erik's room."

"So he's Erik's killer, as well?"

"Yes. After he killed Erik, he took all the music he could find and disappeared. Again, nobody saw him. When he came home, his father noticed something was wrong. Not to mention Jean-Paul had missed his lesson. Alex Waardenburg is the kind of man who doesn't always need words to know what someone else is thinking. This may sound strange, but it is a fact. He didn't have to be a psychic—it didn't take reading his son's thoughts like a book. But he knew something was seriously wrong. He pressed Kiliaan, who told him everything. Alex decided to act. He wanted to save his son *and* the music. He couldn't risk Kiliaan leaving any traces in the boardinghouse. He went there and wiped all possible fingerprints in Erik's room ... and Mina Lyons spotted him."

"How do you explain her silence," wondered Vledder.

DeKok smiled tiredly.

"Mina jumped to the wrong conclusions. She recognized Alex Waardenburg from the television and thought he had killed Erik. The music teacher let her think that. Remember Mina fainting, when I told her about Jean-Paul's murder? She believed she knew the killer ... believed they had an agreement."

Klaver asked: "An agreement? What agreement?"

"When Alex realized he had been discovered, he offered her $10,000 to keep her mouth shut."

"And she accepted?" asked Mrs. DeKok in a horrified tone of voice.

DeKok rubbed his face with a flat hand. He recalled Mina as he had known her in life and in death. He also remembered what Handie Henkie has told him about Mina.

"Certainly," he said after a while. "Alex Waardenburg paid her in cash. When Mina found out, a few days later, how wealthy Waardenburg was, she contacted him again and asked for more money ... $50,000 this time." The grey sleuth shook his head sadly. "She shouldn't have done that. Alex Waardenburg realized she would keep coming back for more. He pretended to agree to her demand, and sent his son to her house. He impressed on Kiliaan the difference between two and three murders was unimportant. They could only hang him once. He forgot we don't have a death penalty anymore. The difference between two and three murders is indeed unimportant, as far as the law is concerned. With the prospect of life imprisonment for multiple murders, Kiliaan really did not care. He went to the boardinghouse and strangled Mina."

DeKok sank back in his chair and remained silent. Then he reached for the bottle to pour again.

"No," interrupted Mrs. DeKok. "First you eat something."

DeKok accepted a tray and selected some particularly appetizing croquettes with mustard. Meanwhile the others replenished themselves from the platters. Mrs. DeKok disappeared to make coffee.

They munched in silence and DeKok refilled the glasses. He remained silent and reviewed the case in his mind once again. It was Klaver who restarted the conversation.

"Now I'm still wondering how you collected that bunch of Irregulars," he complained.

The expression brought another smile to DeKok's face.

"When I had convinced myself," he recommenced, "that Jean-Paul and Erik had been killed because of a stack of music, I was faced with the problem of proving it. There was no tangible evidence. How could I discover who had stolen the melodies, if I didn't even know the melodies?"

"That would have been a problem," said Kuiper thoughtfully. "But you found a solution, didn't you?"

"Yes, I did. After interviewing Ramon Bavel, I

dismissed him as a suspect. Willy Haarveld, as well. As sleazy as he is, I could not see Haarveld as a killer. Of course, he had hired Long Jack and his partner to search the rooms of the two dead boys, but that was *after* the murders ... only after he had read in the papers that the boys had been killed."

"That left the Waardenburgs," guessed Vledder.

"The same old question, after all," observed Kuiper. "Who benefits?"

"That's right. It took me long time to figure out who would benefit from the murders. Waardenburg and Son were the prime suspects, by process of elimination. Even if I had been able to obtain a search warrant for their house, it was unlikely to yield results. So I concentrated on someone with a background in music theory, who would be able to break Jean-Paul's code. It was a question of understanding the principle Jean-Paul used to get his compositions on paper. An advanced music student would be best suited to transcribe the melodies. The graph paper could easily be destroyed later, as has been done, by the way. Again I was left with the Waardenburgs."

"So then you thought of the Irregulars," said Klaver. "But how?"

"It was after some hair tearing on my part. Jean-Paul and Erik used to frequent Little Lowee's bar. It could have been another bar, but Lowee would have known about it, even so. Anyway, Jean-Paul used to give impromptu concerts on half-filled beer glasses in the bar. He became sort of popular and people requested him to play. Since he could read no other music, he played his own melodies," DeKok grinned. "And that was the key. Little Lowee made me a list of the most frequent listeners at those performances."

"The Irregulars."

"Right. After a while the Waardenburgs must have felt a false sense of security. Our investigations were at a complete standstill. To make sure they engaged Willy Haarveld to organize a concert where Kiliaan would appear as soloist on the piano."

"Aha," said his listeners in chorus.

"Aha, indeed. I had waited for such a moment. With Lowee's help we organized the culture club. During the performance, almost all of them recognized the melodies. They had heard them played by Jean-Paul. But this time they were presented as Kiliaan's brain children and it offended them. The show they put on, exceeded my expectations, but it had the desired shock effect."

Inspector Klaver gave DeKok an admiring look.

"It worked brilliantly," he remarked.

"Actually, DeKok," said Kuiper, shaking his head, "you're a louse."

DeKok guffawed.

"You ever hear of a louse that solved murders?"

Kuiper laughed.

"Yes ... today."

ABOUT THE AUTHOR

A. C. Baantjer is one of the most widely read authors in the Netherlands. A former detective inspector of the Amsterdam police, his fictional characters reflect the depth and personality of individuals encountered during his near forty-year-career in law enforcement.

Baantjer was honored with the first-ever Master Prize of the Society of Dutch-language Crime Writers. He was also recently knighted by the Dutch monarchy for his lifetime achievements.

The sixty crime novels featuring Inspector Detective DeKok written by Baantjer have achieved a large following among readers in the Netherlands. A television series, based on these novels, reaches an even wider Dutch audience. Launched nearly a decade ago, the 100th episode of "Baantjer" series recently aired on Dutch channel RTL4.

In large part due to the popularity of the televised "Baantjer" series, sales of Baantjer's novels have increased significantly over the past several years. In 2001, the five millionth copy of his books was sold—a number never before reached by a Dutch author.

Known as the "Dutch Conan Doyle," Baantjer's following continues to grow and conquer new territory. According to the Netherlands Library Information Service, a single copy of a Baanjter title is checked out of a library more than 700,000 times a year.

The DeKok series has been published in China, Russia, Korea, and throughout Europe. Speck Press is pleased to bring you clear and invigorating translations to the English language.

DeKok and the Geese of Death

by Baantjer

Baantjer brings to life Inspector DeKok in another stirring pot-boiler full of suspenseful twists and unusual conclusions.

In *DeKok and The Geese of Death*, DeKok takes on Igor Stablinsky, a man accused of bludgeoning a wealthy old man and his wife. To DeKok's unfailing eye the killing urge is visibly present in the suspect during questioning, but did he commit this particular crime?

All signs point to one of the few remaining estates in Holland. The answer lies within a strange family, suspicions of incest, deadly geese, and a horrifying mansion. Baantjer's perceptive style brings to light the essences of his characters, touching his audience with subtle wit and irony.

"Baantjer has created an odd police detective who roams Amsterdam interacting with the widest possible range of antisocial types. This series is the answer to an insomniac's worst fears."

—*The Boston Globe*

0-9725776-6-1

speck

DeKok and the Death of a Clown

by Baantjer

While investigating a high-stakes jewel theft, Inspector DeKok is called to check out the death of a clown found floating in a raft down the canal, an enormous knife protruding from its back.

Without the slightest trace, a unique, antique jewel collection disappears from a house along the Gentlemen's Canal. As DeKok begins the investigation his assistant, Vledder, receives a call regarding a dead clown at the foot of Crier's Tower. The connection of the crimes initially eludes him, but DeKok's profession, his calling, pushes him towards the answer.

"It's easy to understand the appeal of Amsterdam police detective DeKok."

—*The Los Angeles Times*

0-9725776-9-6

No Laughing Matter

by Peter Guttridge

Tom Sharpe meets Raymond Chandler in *No Laughing Matter* a humorous and brilliant debut that will keep readers on a knife's edge of suspense until the bittersweet end.

When a naked woman flashes past Nick Madrid's hotel window, it's quite a surprise. For Nick's room is on the fourteenth floor, and the hotel doesn't have an outside elevator. The management is horrified when Cissie Parker lands in the swimming pool—not only is she killed, but she makes a real mess of the shallow end.

In Montreal for the Just For Laughs festival, Nick, a journalist who prefers practicing yoga to interviewing the stars, turns gumshoe to answer the question: did she fall or was she pushed? The trail leads first to the mean streets of Edinburgh and then to Los Angeles, where the truth lurks among the dark secrets of Hollywood.

"Guttridge's series is among the funniest and sharpest in the genre, with a level of intelligence often lacking in better-known fare."
—*Balitmore Sun*

0-9725776-4-5

A Ghost of a Chance

by Peter Guttridge

Nick Madrid isn't exactly thrilled when his best friend in journalism, Bridget Frost, commissions him to spend a night in a haunted place on the Sussex Downs and live to tell the tale. Especially as living to tell the tale isn't made an urgent priority.

But Nick stumbles on a hotter story when he discovers a dead man hanging upside down from an ancient oak. Why was he killed? Is there a connection to the nearby New Age conference center? Or to *The Great Beast*, the Hollywood movie about Aleister Crowley, filming down in Brighton?

New Age meets The Old Religion as Nick is bothered, bewildered, but not necessarily bewitched by pagans, satanists, and a host of assorted metaphysicians. Séances, sabbats, a horse-ride from hell, and a kick-boxing zebra all come Nick's way as he obstinately tracks a treasure once in the possession of Crowley.

"… *A Ghost of a Chance* is both funny and clever. This is one of the funniest mysteries to come along in quite a while."

—*Mystery Scene*

0-9725776-8-8

speck

Bullets

by Steve Brewer

When a contract killer bumps off a high roller in a Las Vegas casino, a tangle of romance, gambling, and gunplay follows. The killer, Lily Marsden, is a mysterious and cold woman who is a true professional. But soon, the casino owner, his henchmen, and the victim's two brothers are on Lily's trail.

Throw in some local cops, a playboy, a new widow, a rug merchant, a harridan, and a couple of idiot gamblers named Delbert and Mookie, and the mixture soon boils with intrigue and murder.

"Brewer has created a passel of unique and hilarious characters and thrown them into a page-turning plot that had me laughing out loud despite a hail of bullets."

—*Chicago Sun-Times*

"*Bullets* gives crime fiction fans all the unforgettable characters and fast, fierce action we crave, plus a flavorful overlay of the wry Brewer humor we've come to love. "

—Tony Hillerman

0-9725776-7-X

Boost

by Steve Brewer

Sam Hill steals cars. Not just any cars, but collectible cars, rare works of automotive artistry. Sam's a specialist, and he's made a good life for himself.

But things change after he steals a primo 1965 Thunderbird. In the trunk, Sam finds a corpse, a police informant with a bullet hole between his eyes. Somebody set Sam up. Played a trick on him. And Sam, a prankster himself, can't let it go. He must get his revenge with an even bigger practical joke, one that soon has gangsters gunning for him and police on his tail.

"… entertaining, amusing …. This tightly plotted crime novel packs in a lot of action as it briskly moves along."
—*Chicago Tribune*

"Brewer earns four stars for a clever plot, totally engaging characters, and a pay-back ending … ."
—*Mystery Scene*

0-9725776-5-3 HC | 1-933108-02-9 PB

For a complete catalog of *speck press* books please contact us at the following:

speck press
po box 102004
denver, co 80250, usa
e: books@speckpress.com
t: 800-996-9783
f: 303-756-8011
w: speckpress.com

All of our books are available through your local bookseller.